INDEBTED BRIDE

OLIVIA ASHERS

CHAPTER ONE

Nerea

"THANKS," A GUY SAID as I placed two tall cocktail glasses on the bar in front of him. "Keep the change."

I flashed him a smile that I almost always had plastered on my face when I was working—my boss would probably fire me if I didn't.

As I took the money, I kept my gaze on the guy as he carried the glasses toward a girl in a red dress.

She grinned when he awkwardly handed her one of the glasses, and I sighed, a small smile still curving my lips.

It looked like they were on their first date or something, especially because the guy didn't seem to know what to do with his hands or the glass he was still holding.

When he jerked back because some guy was pushing through the crowd—it was a Saturday night, so Minollis was as packed as ever—he spilled some of his drink on his shirt.

His date laughed and now had just the perfect excuse to run her fingers over his cheek and down his chest.

I had to admit that watching them made me just a teeny tiny bit jealous. I hadn't been on a date in, like, forever.

"Hey, Maria!"

I fought the urge to roll my eyes and grit my teeth when I heard the voice of my least favorite person in the world.

His name was Matt, and he spent his nights sitting at the bar and pestering any girl who was unlucky enough to cross his path.

And, unfortunately, I couldn't run away or tell him to

fuck off. I could try to do the latter, but I might lose my job.

I'd seen Matt shake hands with my boss once, and I suspected they were friends.

Good friends.

If I complained about Matt, I'd probably be the one to get kicked out, and I couldn't afford that.

Jobs weren't easy to come by.

"My name is Nerea," I said as I slowly turned to Matt, forcing my lips into a smile. "Neh-reh-a."

I'd always been proud of the fact that my mom had named me after my great-grandmother who'd lived in Bilbao, Spain, but if I had a nickel for every time someone mispronounced, misheard, misspelled, or completely got my name wrong, I'd be rich.

"Do you want another beer?" I asked because Matt was just looking at me with his glassy dark eyes.

His hand shot out, covering mine on the bar, and I wasn't quick enough to pull away.

"What are you doing tonight?" He cocked his head.

"Working, obviously."

"Later," he slurred.

"That's none of your business." I pulled my hand out from under his, and he frowned. "Sorry, Matt. I'm busy."

I was grateful for the guy who waved at me, and I hurried to get his order.

A groan escaped my throat when I saw the bottle I'd just picked up was empty, so I headed to the storage room to get a new one.

I searched through the boxes, and when I finally spotted the bottle I was looking for, I bent to pick it up.

Hands wrapped around my waist, and I yelped as someone rubbed themselves against my ass.

My heart jumped into my throat, and I quickly spun around, trying to shove the person who'd grabbed me off me.

"It's just me," Matt said with a big grin on his face.

My chest heaved.

"You can't be here!" My gaze darted to the door, which was behind Matt's back.

I had to get past him.

Now.

But as soon as I took a step forward, he got in my way, his broad shoulders blocking my path.

"Matt, I need to get back to work, and you can't be in here," I said, keeping my voice steady.

"Oh, come on, Maria. I know you want me," he breathed, getting closer to me.

He reeked of alcohol, and yeah, I'd had to serve him all that alcohol, so I doubted he could think clearly. Not that he was any better when he wasn't drunk.

"You're drunk, and you're wrong. I'm not

interested in you." I planted my hands firmly on his chest, but he was too strong, and I couldn't push him away.

"We can meet later," he said, his hands landing on my waist. "I know where you live."

My eyes widened.

What the fuck?

So he wasn't just a drunk but also a stalker? He must've followed me home after work.

And yet, he couldn't even get my name right.

Did I even want to know what this creep really wanted from me and what kind of fantasy he'd come up with in his head?

Shit!

"I..." I tilted my head, trying not to show him that my skin was crawling from his touch.

His lips lowered toward mine. I kept my gaze on his, and then I stepped on his foot as hard as I could.

He stumbled back with a surprised yelp, and I used his distraction and broke into a run.

"Maria, wait!"

I didn't stop or look back. As I got out of the storage room, my eyes quickly scanned the room. I should call the cops.

My phone.

Where the hell was my phone?

I spotted it just as Matt got out of the storage room too. The phone was right behind him.

Fuck!

I looked around. Everyone was drinking or having fun.

Surely, Matt wouldn't try anything in front of all these people.

But he started toward me anyway.

Maybe there was a way to stop him.

If I could convince him that I had a boyfriend, he might leave me alone, and I wouldn't have to risk potentially losing my job.

Not to mention creeps like Matt rarely gave up so easily, and the cops wouldn't be able to do much, except maybe give him a restraining order that might make him angry and even more intent on getting to me.

My gaze fell on the tattoo on Matt's neck. One of the girls who worked in the other shift had told me it was a gang tattoo, but I had no idea if she was right. If she was, getting rid of Matt just might turn out to be even more difficult than I thought.

I backed away from Matt, scanning the crowd. If I accidentally "stole" some girl's boyfriend, that might end up messy.

Alone.

I had to find some guy who was alone.

A dark-haired man in a suit who was sitting at the table in the corner caught my eye. He was alone, and there were only other men around him.

He was also very handsome and definitely looked strong enough to be able to fight off someone like Matt. I doubted Matt would be dumb enough to pick a fight with another guy over me.

"Maria—"

"My boyfriend's here!" I said to Matt.

Maybe just hearing the word *boyfriend* would be enough for him to realize I didn't want to be with him, since me saying I wasn't interested in him clearly wasn't enough for him for some reason.

"What?" His brow furrowed as if he couldn't understand what I'd just said. "You don't have—"

I rushed toward the stranger.

When I glanced over my shoulder, Matt was right behind me.

Fuck!

He didn't believe me, did he?

"I'm so sorry, but I really need you to pretend to be my boyfriend," I blurted out as I straddled the stranger, wrapping my arms around his neck with a smile on my face.

The stranger's blue eyes lifted to me, sparkling with amusement, as a smile spread across his lips. His arms wound around me just as Matt came to a stop with a puzzled look on his face.

The stranger's smile faded as he turned his head toward Matt.

Matt's eyes went wide, his mouth hanging open, and he stumbled back.

And then he broke into a run, pushing through the crowd like a madman.

What the hell had just happened?

I focused my attention back on the stranger.

I'd expected Matt might give up, but I hadn't expected he'd be running away as if his life depended on it.

The stranger lifted his hand, and I glanced at the men dressed in black who were occupying the two tables next to his.

They looked like they were about to get up, but they sat back down, and I caught a glimpse of a gun under the jacket of one of them.

Oh shit.

Had I made a huge mistake?

Were these guys some gang members too?

"He'll never bother you again," the stranger said, his piercing eyes trained on mine.

"Thank you. I'm really sorry I just—" I tried to get up, but the stranger held me in a tight grip.

"You owe me a favor now," he said coldly.

"Um, if you want another drink, I'll—"

"No, not a drink. I just saved you from that idiot." He leaned closer. "I don't do anything for free," he whispered into my ear, and a shudder ran down my spine.

"What do you want?" I swallowed past the lump forming in my throat.

"I'll find you once I need you." He let go of me, and I pushed myself up to my feet.

As I strode away from him, I glanced back.

His gaze was still trained on me, a small smile quirking the corners of his lips.

Whoever this guy was, he just might be even worse than Matt.

What the hell had I gotten myself into?

I spotted the guy who was still waiting for his drink. "I'm sorry. I'll get your drink right away."

"It's okay. I wouldn't want to get on *his* bad side." The guy glanced in the direction of the mysterious stranger.

"Do you know who he is?"

The guy leaned closer. "Don't you know?"

I shook my head.

The guy grimaced. "They say he's a mafia boss, but if anyone asks, you didn't hear it from me."

I blinked at him.

I'd thrown myself in the arms of a mafia boss?

Oh, for fuck's sake!

Was everyone a criminal in this shitty place? Or was I just so damn unlucky?

But he'd seemed so damn... safe.

Now what should I do?

I had no idea.

CHAPTER TWO

"HOW WAS YOUR NIGHT?" Romano asked as I entered the room and took a seat in one of the chairs.

"Interesting." The image of the hot bartender with dark brown eyes and long dark brown hair who'd unexpectedly straddled me flashed through my mind.

She'd thought I'd save her from that jerk for free, but I'd learned a long time ago that no one would ever just help anyone without expecting something in return. So why would I do it?

Her gratefulness meant nothing to me and would never help me in my goal to rule this city and become an even better boss than my father.

But a favor, even from a seemingly insignificant pretty little bartender, might come in handy one day.

"I know you have something important to say, so speak," I said, meeting Romano's dark gaze.

He was my advisor and my second-in-command, and probably the only person who I trusted enough to actually consider his advice.

He'd been by my side from the day I was born.

"Yes, it's about the Catrona deal," he said, running a hand through his graying brown hair. "My contacts tell me the board members are seriously thinking about giving the deal to Vitrianni."

I laughed. "Are you fucking kidding me?"

What could my biggest enemy offer them that I couldn't?

Absolutely nothing, and my company would do a way better job of building a new hotel complex for the Catrona hotel chain.

The person who won that deal would have all the

doors open for them after that. Everyone would want to work with them.

It would create new business opportunities, even overseas, and it would be just perfect for money laundering.

"I know how you can sway them," Romano said.

I raised an eyebrow at him.

"You should get married."

I snorted. "Yeah, right. Because me being married is the most important thing here."

"There are rumors about you, Oliver." Romano's gaze was trained on mine. "Yes, it's just rumors and no one has any proof, but even rumors can be dangerous. If you showed the board members that you're a family man, they might be less likely to believe those rumors."

"That's fucking ridiculous."

"It is, but you know most of the board members are dinosaurs who care a lot about appearances. Vitrianni has a family and a wife he adores. He presents himself as a family man, and everyone's more likely to trust someone like him with their business."

"Vitrianni's pretending."

Love didn't exist, and Vitrianni knew that well.

"He might be, yes," Romano said. "But that's exactly what he needs, and it's working, while everyone knows you've never had a serious relationship. Vitrianni might be fucking a different woman every night, but he's showing the world a different image of himself, and you should do the same."

I pressed my lips into a tight line.

Pretending to be someone else had never been my thing, but I was willing to do anything to reach my goal.

Even if it was something unpleasant that I had no desire to do.

Sacrifices had to be made if I wanted to get everything I wanted.

"All right. I'll consider it," I said.

"It's not just about appearances either. You need heirs. Your father had you very late, and he had to wait with his retirement. A lot of things could've happened. Your position will be much stronger and secure if your enemies know you have plenty of heirs. And there's another opportunity you should consider. An alliance. Marriages can unite families. I pulled up a list of families with daughters—"

I furrowed my brow.

Getting married was one thing, but having heirs and getting involved with another mafia family wasn't something I wanted to deal with right now.

If I died, I wouldn't give a fuck about the one who got to rule after me.

I needed something less permanent. A wife who'd

exist just to help me with the family man image so the idiot board members would take me seriously.

I didn't want a girl who'd be like my mother—having a child she hadn't been ready for, for all the wrong reasons.

But where could I find a woman willing to play along? Someone who I could trust?

I could pay someone for the job, but she might be a risk if she found out too much about me.

Even signing a non-disclosure agreement sometimes wasn't enough to stop people from talking to the press or the cops. Threats didn't always work out with certain people either.

It had to be someone who'd be afraid of me enough not to dare to talk.

Someone who owed me a favor.

I smiled.

"Have you already made a choice?" Romano asked.

I'd stopped listening to him. He must've read me a list of some of the acceptable families for an arranged marriage and thought I liked one of the options.

"Yes. I need you to find out everything about the pretty bartender who works at Minollis. I saw her last night."

"What?" Romano blinked at me.

"She owes me a favor."

"I don't understand how that—"

"You don't need to understand. Just get everything you can find on her. Now."

"All right." Romano inclined his head, confusion still filling his eyes, but he knew better than to ask me for an explanation.

When it was time for him to know what I'd decided, I'd tell him.

The bartender could be a solution to my problem.

She'd looked scared enough of me and clueless too. It would be easy to get from her whatever I wanted.

Once Romano was gone, I got to my feet and headed to the table with drinks in the corner of the room. After I poured myself a glass of whiskey, I went out onto the terrace.

Peace and quiet.

Just perfect.

When I heard the door open, I glanced over my shoulder. Romano was already back. He'd been away for maybe half an hour.

"What?" I asked when he reached me.

"I forgot to mention another benefit of having a family."

My eyebrows shot up.

"You'd have someone to talk to other than me, and

you wouldn't spend hours drinking alone or in your office."

"Are you saying I'm an alcoholic?"

"That can't be the only thing you heard."

"I like being alone."

It made things less complicated.

I didn't need anyone anyway.

I could do whatever the fuck I wanted when I wanted it. Why would I waste my precious time on a wife or a child?

No benefits for me at all.

"Here's everything I could find on your bartender." He pulled out his phone and handed it to me. "Her name is Nerea Simmons. I think she's the one you were talking about. The other one is blonde, so I guess not your type."

I glanced at the photo on the screen. "It's her."

Nerea.

Beautiful name, but not as beautiful as she was.

"There's not much about her. She's an ordinary girl. Twenty-one. Living alone. No family."

"No family?" Now, that would make my plan ridiculously easy.

"Her parents passed away in a house fire when she was a child. She lived with her grandparents after that."

"And her grandparents—"

"Both dead. If she has any other relatives, they don't live here."

"Perfect." I scrolled through the info.

I knew how to get Nerea to agree to be my wife.

I didn't believe in fate, but if there was some higher force out there, it wanted me to rule the city.

I was sure of it.

And Nerea was going to give me what I needed.

CHAPTER THREE

Nerea

I HADN'T SEEN MATT or the stranger in the past few days, and I hoped it would stay that way. The last thing I needed was to get entangled in some mafia drama that I knew nothing about.

Wrapping my jacket tighter around myself, I quickened my steps as I strode down the street. Minollis had just closed, and my apartment was only a few blocks away.

The roar of car engines filled the air. Very often, some rich kids used this street for racing. It was just my luck that they'd decided to do it tonight too.

I had to hurry and get out of here.

Somewhere safer.

Not that any of the dark alleys would feel safer, but I didn't want to end up splattered like a pancake on the sidewalk because some dumb kid lost control of his car.

Tires screeched just behind my back, and when I looked in the direction of the noise, my breath got caught in my chest.

A van had pulled over, and masked men jumped out. They started toward me and caught me by the arms before I could break into a run.

I opened my mouth to scream, but one of the men covered my mouth with something thick. Only muffled sounds escaped my throat as I thrashed against their strong grip.

Black spots danced in my vision, and I felt my body go limp.

Too bad no one was going to miss me, or even realize I was gone until it was time for my shift.

And by then, it would probably be too late.

I CRACKED MY EYES OPEN, my head throbbing.

But as soon as I realized I was in a dim, empty room and tied to a chair, I was wide awake and my heart was thudding like crazy.

When I lifted my gaze, I spotted a camera in the corner of the room.

No matter how much I tried, I couldn't free myself.

A few moments later, the door opened.

A man walked in, followed by two armed guys.

Once he got closer, I recognized his cold blue eyes.

The stranger from Minollis.

The mafia boss.

He strolled toward me, the sleeves of his white dress shirt rolled up and revealing the strong muscles of his arms.

"Hello, Nerea," he said with a smile.

The way my name rolled off his tongue with ease almost had me impressed, but I was tied to a chair after getting kidnapped, so it was hard to care.

"My name is Oliver Gavellini," he said. "I'm sorry about this."

Except, there was absolutely nothing showing on his face or in his eyes that would indicate that he was even a tiny bit sorry.

"What do you want?" I asked, and licked my dry lips.

"I have an offer for you. You owe me a favor. I came to collect, and if you accept my offer, you'll earn some extra cash too."

Oh shit.

Was he going to ask me to sell drugs for him or something?

Oh no!

What if he wanted me to kill someone for him? If he expected me to slip something into someone's drink—

"I want you to marry me and be my wife for five years," he said.

My jaw hit the floor.

I had to be hallucinating.

There was no way I'd just gotten kidnapped by a mafia boss, only for him to offer me to become his wife.

"You'll get three million dollars once our contract is complete," he added.

Three million—

Was he messing with me?

With all that money, it would be so easy to fulfill the promise I'd made to my grandma.

I wouldn't have to be saving money for a trip to Bilbao so I could find my relatives and give them the stuff my grandma wanted them to have. She'd insisted I had to do it in person.

But I couldn't think about the money.

Oliver pulled out a knife and headed toward me. My heart jumped into my throat, and I was barely breathing when he reached me.

His gaze regarded me with cold interest as he cut through my restraints.

I rubbed my wrists, watching him carefully as he put away the knife.

He could kill me.

It would mean nothing to him.

But why me?

Why did he want me to be his wife? It didn't make any sense.

"I... Um..." I didn't know what to say.

"You'd have to live with me and always be at my disposal. I have enemies who'd want you dead, so you can't be on your own. For five years, you're mine, and after, you'll be free. I'll get you a new identity. You're only twenty-one. Five years will seem like nothing to you, and then you'll have everything you could've ever possibly dreamed of."

His penetrating gaze was trained on me, and it felt as if he could see straight into my soul. My stomach clenched into a tight ball.

"And if I refuse?" I choked out.

"Then you'll still owe me a favor, but you might not like the thing I ask for next." He grinned.

I glanced at the men who were at the door.

If I refused, he might as well kill me right here, right now.

He hadn't dragged me all the way here just to let me go without getting anything.

One look at him, and I could tell he was used to getting whatever he wanted. I couldn't believe I'd missed that air of arrogance around him the first time I saw him.

"But what about my job and my apartment? I have to —" I should just shut up and agree to whatever the hell he wanted so I could survive this, and yet, I couldn't stop myself.

I was probably just stalling because this wasn't an easy decision.

Not for me, anyway.

"It's not a problem. You won't need a job because you'll have everything you need, and I can have someone take care of your apartment. But bear in mind that any special requests you might have will cost you and come out of your three million. Our deal will be a secret, and you're not allowed to even breathe a word of anything concerning me and our arrangement to anyone. If you do, bad things will happen to you and you'll owe me a whole lot of money, and trust me, you don't want that."

The dangerous glint in his eyes made me flinch.

"All right." I didn't really have a choice, and if he needed me alive, that was good.

I'd come up with something to get myself out of this mess somehow.

There had to be a way.

"There's one thing you have to do first, before we sign the agreement," he said.

"What's that?"

"I'll take you to my doctor for a checkup. I need to know you're worth my investment."

I narrowed my gaze at him.

Investment?

Wow.

This guy was a real piece of work.

He didn't give a damn about anything as long as he got what he wanted.

But why did he need a wife?

"Get up," he said. "You're coming with me."

I pushed myself up to my feet.

He just wasn't going to explain anything else, was he?

Not even what else he expected from me.

I supposed I'd find out soon enough.

ONCE EVERYTHING WAS signed and done, I brought Nerea to my house. The surprised look on her face as she looked around was entertaining.

Her shitty old apartment was nothing compared to this.

A room in this house was bigger than her whole

apartment, and I only had the best: the most modern and expensive furniture, and the latest of gadgets and equipment.

If Nerea thought she'd be able to escape this place, she was wrong.

My men watched the house carefully, and I had plenty of alarms in place to prevent anyone from getting in or out without my permission.

Romano appeared in the foyer, narrowing his gaze at Nerea. The tightness around his mouth told me that he didn't like her and wasn't happy about my decision, but I didn't care.

I always did what was best for me.

And Nerea was exactly what I needed.

"Romano, make an announcement about my wedding so that the board members find out about it," I said.

He inclined his head. "Do you want me to take your future wife to one of the guest rooms?"

It would be easy to send Nerea to the other side of the house and forget that she was even here.

But I wanted to see her.

She was pretty, and I had to keep an eye on her.

There were three more empty rooms on my private floor. She could stay in one.

If she entered my room by mistake and found her way into my bed, I wouldn't mind at all.

She was more than fuckable, and just the thought of having her body under mine made my balls tighten.

Should I even have such a distraction so close to me?

But she was going to be my wife, so I'd have to get to know her, or people would get suspicious.

"Come," I said.

Nerea followed me upstairs.

Her curious gaze wandered around. It was a surprise she hadn't begged me to let her go.

She hadn't even cried or tried to pester me with a billion questions.

I liked that about her.

"This is your room," I said, opening the door. "Everything you need will be brought to you. As long as you do what I want you to do, you have nothing to worry about."

She lifted her chin, crossing her arms, a defiant gaze in her dark eyes. "As long as what you want is within reason."

A smile spread across my lips. "I always get what I want. Don't forget that."

She watched me for a few moments, and then she entered her room. "Is that all?"

"For now."

She slammed the door closed.

I chuckled.

Nerea had more fight in her than I'd thought.

Definitely entertaining.

But she'd bend to my will, just like everyone else.

Nerea

I SAT DOWN ON THE HUGE bed and looked around.

The room was awesome, just like the whole house. It was very spacious, had its own bathroom and a terrace, and had an amazing closet ornamented with carved roses.

But it was nothing more than a fancy prison.

I buried my face in my hands.

What should I do now?

I'd signed an agreement with Oliver and I was going to become his wife, but I still didn't know anything about him or about what he really expected from me.

The contract stated that I'd have to do what he said, and that any major violations of our deal could terminate the whole thing, which would be bad for me because I'd owe him for all the damage done.

It didn't say anywhere he'd kill me, but I hadn't had the time to take a closer look and read between the lines.

Maybe I should've brought a lawyer with me before signing anything, but I doubted Oliver would've allowed me to do that, and besides, lawyers cost money, which I didn't have.

At least not until the contract ended and I divorced Oliver.

But Oliver was a mafia boss. Was a piece of paper really going to mean anything to him?

Maybe, if he had a code of honor.

It was possible I'd made a huge mistake by agreeing to any of this, but I didn't think he would've let me go just like that, especially because I knew he needed a fake wife and could've told someone about it.

I got to my feet and went out onto the terrace.

As I gazed around, all I could see were trees and endless fields. But if I tried to run, I'd have to go through all the armed guards and a fence.

It seemed impossible.

If Oliver caught me trying to escape, he'd probably kill me.

Would being his wife be anything like being a real wife? I read something about a wife of a mafia boss in the newspaper once, and if any of it had been real, I didn't think I'd want to be treated that way.

But what was I to Oliver anyway?

An investment, he'd said.

Like a piece of property.

Something not human.

I shuddered and hugged myself. There had to be a way out of this.

There had to be something I could do, because I didn't think Oliver would just let me go in five years. Who knew if there'd be anything left of me in five years anyway?

Living with him was dangerous. Someone else might try to kill me.

I looked up at the sky.

My grandma had told me that I should have a lot of friends who'd be there for me once she was gone. If only I'd listened.

But I'd been the quiet girl who'd gotten teased at school, and when my grandma had needed me to take care of her before she'd passed, I hadn't had any time to hang out with my rare friends.

Eventually, everyone had stopped inviting me to things, and we'd drifted apart.

Oliver had made me sign a resignation letter for my boss, so no one would think it was weird if I didn't show for work. My neighbors were going to think I'd gone off somewhere or finally gotten myself a better job.

I didn't know if anyone would realize I was going to marry Oliver. Maybe he was well known in business circles, but I'd never heard of him before.

Would the news of our wedding be in the newspapers? On TV? Or did he only want his family to think he'd finally settled?

Oliver had told me so little I didn't even know what I'd gotten myself into.

All he'd cared about was making sure I wouldn't spill his secrets or whatever I found out about him and that I did as he said.

But if he needed a pretend wife, then it had to be for a reason. I might be able to go out. If I disappeared and Oliver couldn't find me, I could save myself.

I rushed inside.

Maybe there was another way to find out who Oliver

was, or at least I could find something more about him —about his legit business.

It all had to be online.

I didn't have a TV, or a laptop, or a phone in my room, so I headed out into the hallway. Maybe there was a room with computers, or something.

I wasn't Oliver's captive, right?

I quietly moved through the hallway, checking the rooms that were unlocked. When I spotted a phone, I rushed to it.

Access denied.

It was written on the screen as my hand touched it.

Shit!

I found a tablet in another room, but it was locked too.

Everything was locked, and not responding to my fingerprint because it wasn't in the system.

My chest constricted.

I *was* Oliver's captive.

He'd cut me off from the world. I couldn't call anyone or contact anyone, even if I wanted to.

Maybe he'd let me make a call if I asked him nicely, but then he'd know everything I said.

Would he even allow me to get in touch with the outside world? Would he let me browse the internet? Or did he consider all that a security risk?

Of course he hadn't mentioned any of that to me.

Not that it would've changed anything.

He was a mafia boss, and I should be figuring out a way to get away from him as soon as possible, before he dragged me into his shit.

If he got arrested for whatever bad things he was undoubtedly doing, I could go down with him as his accomplice or something.

But we weren't married yet.

If he wanted to throw a wedding party, maybe I could use it and slip away.

And then I'd have to run as fast and as far away as possible because I was sure he'd try to hunt me down, and he wouldn't show me any mercy.

CHAPTER SIX

"WE HAVE A PROBLEM," Romano said as he entered my office.

"What now?"

"The announcement of your wedding caught some unexpected attention."

"What do you mean?"

"There's a reporter who wrote an article about you and your wife-to-be. It's not good."

"A reporter?" I frowned. "Who?"

"His name is Clive Willis. He has quite a following."

"Never heard of him. What does he say?"

"He says that it's suspicious that you're suddenly getting married when no one has seen you with Nerea before. He apparently spoke to her neighbors who said they knew nothing about her having a boyfriend, and that they haven't seen you visit her. He also somehow took a few photos of you bringing Nerea here. He interpreted the expression on her face as worried and scared, and he's using that to fuel the rumors about you."

"Why is he even writing about me? I'm not a celebrity."

"But you were on the list of the youngest and most successful businessmen, and you even made it to the most desirable bachelor list in one popular magazine. I haven't told you about it because you said you didn't care. But that was apparently enough for the reporter to think there's a story worth telling. Something that would grab attention."

"Kill him," I said.

"I don't believe that would be a good move. We don't know much about Clive because he wasn't on our radar before, but not everyone would dare to write an article about someone like you, especially if he believes the rumors are true. Let me investigate. If we kill him now, even if it's deemed an accident, the consequences could be catastrophic. You need to quell the rumors, not add more fire to the flames."

I gritted my teeth. "All right. Investigate him. Tell whoever runs that damn paper that I'm going to sue them for spreading lies and upsetting my future wife."

"It wouldn't be a bad idea if we could get Clive to change his tune and write something that's going to help you, but only if we see that he doesn't have anyone's protection and isn't working with one of your enemies."

"Someone could've paid him to say that bullshit. He might not know some of the rumors about me are true."

"I don't know, but for now, I think it's important to show the world, and especially to those who want to give the Catrona deal to your enemy, that you and your fiancée are very much in love and that she's happy about the wedding."

"Issue a statement then."

"No, not a statement. That wouldn't be enough. An interview with Nerea would work better."

I raised an eyebrow at him. "Why? Just because some piece of shit of a reporter sprouted some lies about me? Reporters lie and invent things all the time. Everyone knows that. They twist the truth and come up with clickbait headlines to get their stupid paper to sell."

"Yes, but you're getting married for a reason, and you don't want anyone to just ruin all your hard work. We can record an interview with Nerea on our own and then sell it to some magazine. To someone who won't have a problem with the narrative."

"All right. Let's do that. Set everything up."

Romano dipped his head. "But Nerea has to be convincing, or none of this will work."

"She'll do fine."

Fucking this up wasn't an option, and that damn reporter was going to learn not to mess with me.

CHAPTER SEVEN

Nerea

I PACED UP AND DOWN the room, unable to stop my racing mind.

As soon as one of Oliver's men had told me I had to get ready because I was supposed to do an interview, I couldn't stop worrying.

If I had to do an interview, then many people would see

it, and everyone would see my face. If I ran away, Oliver was going to be super pissed off, and it would be easier for him to find me if anyone on the street could recognize me.

But I couldn't think about that right now. I had to stay strong.

Maybe I could finally talk to Oliver and he'd tell me what he really expected from me. Maybe it wouldn't be so bad if all I had to do was fake being his wife when he needed it and if he left me alone otherwise.

A knock sounded on the door, making me jump. Only a moment later, Oliver cracked it open.

Now was my chance.

I could ask him what I needed to ask, and I could refuse to do the interview until he explained everything to me.

But his face was deadly serious, his eyes flashing with annoyance. A gun was tucked in the holster around his waist.

I opened my mouth, but instead of saying something, I bit down on my lip.

Maybe now wasn't the time to talk to him.

He was already angry. It was coming off him in waves.

"Are you ready?" His gaze traveled my body, and I suddenly felt naked in the pink dress I'd put on, but it had been the only thing I could find that seemed decent enough for an interview.

"Um, yeah."

"Good." He offered me a sheet of paper that I hadn't even noticed he'd been holding. "This is all you have to say."

I took the paper and quickly scanned through it. From what I could see, I was supposed to convince everyone I loved Oliver more than anything else in the whole world.

That wasn't going to be easy.

I barely even knew him, and any feelings I could possibly have for him weren't nice at all.

"Come," he said, and headed for the door.

"Am I supposed to memorize this?" I asked as I hurried after him.

"No. My guys are recording, so you only have to read one sentence and repeat it while looking into the camera."

"Why do I have to do this?"

His gaze met mine. "Does it matter?"

"I'd like to know."

"Because I need you to do it."

Well, isn't that just great, Mr. Not-Helpful-At-All?

Oliver led me to a room on the other side of the

house. It was full of cameras and recording equipment, and there was a black chair in the middle.

"Sit," Oliver said.

I settled in the chair. A beam of light was pointed at me, nearly blinding me, and then the cameras moved closer.

Just how many different angles of me did he need for this interview?

My throat was dry, and I clutched the paper with my answers tightly in my hand.

"Let's begin," a dark-haired, dark-eyed guy said as he approached.

He immediately read the first question and didn't even bother introducing himself to me or giving me any helpful tips or instructions.

Maybe he thought Oliver had already explained everything, or maybe Oliver surrounded himself with people who were exactly like him.

I glanced down at the paper, and then I looked up into the camera.

"Hi, I'm ... um, Nerea Simmons."

"No," the guy said, shaking his head. "You're supposed to sound confident and smile. Try to relax, okay?"

"Okay," I said as I glanced at Oliver, who was lounging against the wall, his intent gaze on me.

How the hell was I supposed to relax when a mafia boss was watching me like that?

I tried again, but this time, I ended up coughing. "Can I get some water, please?"

"Sure." The guy grabbed a bottle of water and tossed it to me.

I took a few sips and lowered the bottle to the floor next to my chair.

Plastering a big smile on my face, like I'd done so many times at Minollis, I focused on the camera. "Hi, I'm Nerea Simmons, and I—"

The guy shook his head again. "Now you sound like you're trying to sell something. Not natural enough."

I groaned.

Well, I *was* trying to sell something, wasn't I? Why would that be a problem?

I read my sentence again, but some of my annoyance seeped into my voice.

"Stop," Oliver said, pushing himself off the wall.

I froze as he strode toward me. He stopped just behind my back, his hands landing on my shoulders.

I could barely breathe as his fingers dug into my skin, and his lips brushed my ear as he leaned forward.

"Think about all the money you're going to earn for this," he said, rubbing my shoulders. "Think about all the things you're going to do when this is over."

When he let go of me, I swallowed hard.

It was easy for him to say that, but I couldn't think about something that might or might not happen in five years.

Actually, thinking that I might be stuck with him for five years scared me to death.

I lifted my gaze to the camera again. "Hi, I'm—"

"We're taking a break," Oliver said and caught my arm. "Come."

The sheet of paper I'd been holding flew out of my hand and landed on the floor.

I got to my feet, my pulse speeding up. "Where are you taking me? I can do this. I just need a few more tries and—"

"You look like someone's holding a gun to your head." He let go of me as we reached the hallway.

"Can you blame me for that?" I lowered my gaze to his gun, my voice laced with annoyance.

I should probably keep quiet, but I couldn't.

Maybe I'd do better without him in the room.

He only looked at me, and then motioned for me to follow him.

I trailed after him down the hallway. Where was he taking me?

We reached a door at the end of the hallway, and he opened it wide for me.

I entered, my brow furrowing when I saw a big Jacuzzi in the middle of the room.

"When I want to relax after a long day, I come here. You'll feel better. Get in."

"But I'm wearing a dress and I—"

He caught the zipper and tugged it down. "There's an easy solution for that."

His fingers brushed the bare skin of my back, and a shudder ran through me.

"I don't have a bathing suit, and I'm not getting in there naked." I met his gaze.

"You don't have to be naked." A smile tilted his lips. "I'll be back."

He left the room, leaving me alone.

What should I do?

My underwear was black, and I supposed it wasn't going to expose me any more than a bikini would, but should I just do what Oliver said, even if this wasn't something he actually needed from me?

I eyed the Jacuzzi.

I'd never done this before, and a part of me was curious.

Eyeing the door, I let my dress slip to the floor.

I stepped out of it and kicked off my shoes. When I dipped my toes into the water, it was nicely warm, so I got in.

I sat down, letting the water embrace me.

Oh hell.

It felt so damn nice.

Comforting, in a weird way.

I leaned my head back and sighed.

But then the door opened, and all the tension was back when Oliver returned.

He placed something—a large metal container—on the table that was in the corner. After he pulled something out of the container, I watched him carefully as he got closer.

He offered me a glass of red wine, and I took it.

"I don't know if I should be drinking—" I said.

"A sip or two won't hurt."

Maybe he was right.

I took a sip.

Damn, the wine tasted amazing. Where the hell had he gotten it? But I supposed someone like him only had access to the best.

"Do you like it?" he asked.

"It's good."

"Close your eyes."

"Why?" I gave him a questioning look.

He got closer, rolling the sleeves of his dress shirt up. "Just do it."

I met his gaze.

Was he going to hurt me?

I didn't think so. Doing that would mess up the interview for sure.

His face was no longer serious, and there was something else in his gaze now.

After some hesitation, I closed my eyes.

"Don't open them," he said softly, and I heard him shifting closer to me.

A yelp escaped my throat when something cold pressed against my cheek.

"Shh. Relax," he whispered as he slid what had to be an ice cube down my cheek and to my neck.

I gasped as he trailed the ice over my skin.

Hot.

Cold.

It was a powerful mix.

I shuddered as he dipped the ice between my breasts.

But it felt strangely good.

The tension seeped out of my shoulders, and when the ice melted, Oliver's cold fingers glided down my arm.

I opened my eyes, my gaze finding his.

He was watching me with something in his eyes that looked like curiosity, or maybe desire. His lips pulled up into a small smile.

"Better?" he asked.

I could only nod.

"You and I will do the interview. I'll ask the questions, and you'll answer, as if you were talking to a friend."

"Okay." I took another sip of the wine.

It was a surprise I hadn't spilled it.

But I was way more relaxed now, and I somehow cared less about the stupid interview.

"I THINK I'M THE LUCKIEST woman in the whole world," Nerea said with a smile, and let out a small laugh.

"Perfect," I said, pushing the camera out of the way.

Nerea had successfully completed the interview, and

now all my men had to do was edit the video to make it look as convincing as possible.

Nerea's smile faded, and her gaze met mine.

She might look innocent and sweet, but there was fire simmering under the surface. Her eyes were full of it, even if she didn't always let it show.

She wasn't like any of the women that often surrounded me. Her eyes were filled with life, despite the circumstances, and she didn't have that look of despair that seemed to cling to many mafia women.

She also didn't strike me as one of those mafia wives who did everything to look as sexy as possible and went on shopping sprees whenever they could.

But Nerea hadn't been raised to become the wife of a mafia boss.

She was just an ordinary bartender.

A girl who'd stumbled into my life by pure chance.

It had taken all my willpower to stop touching her in that Jacuzzi. I'd wanted to get in there with her and fuck her until she couldn't think about anything else.

But she was only a pretty distraction.

Nothing else.

Once we were married, I'd find a way to get from her what I wanted, and then I'd only have to see her if we had to go together somewhere.

No one could hold my interest forever.

She would be no different.

"Can we talk?" she asked, tucking a few strands of her hair behind her ear.

"Not now. I'm busy."

Disappointment crossed her face, but I had a good guess about what she wanted to ask. She had to have questions about our arrangement, and she'd finally dared to ask, but she'd have to wait.

I didn't want her to think that something had changed, or that we'd be friends who'd waste their time on useless conversations.

I didn't do anything that didn't benefit me.

If she hadn't realized that by now, she would figure it out soon.

I gave her one more look, and then I headed out.

CHAPTER NINE

I TOOK A DEEP BREATH before getting out of the bathroom. Tonight was my wedding rehearsal, and just thinking about it felt so damn weird.

I didn't know if Oliver had rented the restaurant we were at or if he owned it, but the whole place had been set up just for us and surrounded by guards, who watched everything like hawks, so it was hard to figure out if there was a way out for me.

When I stepped out into the hallway, a blonde in a silver dress smiled at me.

"You're going to follow this path," she said, pointing at the floor and the narrow red carpet that led into a huge room.

"Um, okay," I said, glad that I wasn't already wearing my wedding dress, but just a plain black cocktail dress instead.

I did have to wear my wedding shoes because I had to get used to walking in them.

There were so many cameras everywhere, and I couldn't help but feel a little bit nervous about the whole thing.

"How many people are going to be at the wedding?" I asked the woman.

If Oliver didn't want to tell me anything, maybe she would.

"About five hundred," she said, and my eyes widened. "That's not including the press and reporters."

"So there are going to be lots of reporters?"

"Yes," she said. "It's going to be a huge event."

"Why is everyone so interested in this wedding?"

She furrowed her brow. "Why wouldn't they be?"

We entered the room where the wedding was

supposed to take place. There was a huge chandelier with tons of shiny crystals above our heads, and the room was completely in golden tones.

There were plenty of tables and chairs, and at the end of the room, Oliver stood with a dark-haired man, who I supposed was the one who'd be conducting the ceremony.

"Just follow the red carpet and don't forget to smile," the woman said. "Remember that all eyes are going to be on you. Every girl out there will want to be in your place."

Yeah, sure.

Absolutely everyone would love to marry a mafia boss and be his fake wife.

It sounded like a dream come true.

Not.

"Slow down," the woman instructed. "Listen to the music. Follow its beat. Look only at Oliver and no one else."

Oliver focused on me when he saw me approaching.

My heart rate quickened under his intense gaze, and I already wanted to turn around and run away, even if this wasn't the real thing.

But I forced myself to keep going.

"Smile," the woman said.

Right.

Ugh.

I forced my lips into a small smile as I kept walking.

"Stand over there." The woman pointed at the spot right across from Oliver.

I did as she asked and found myself face-to-face with Oliver.

He watched me with amusement in his eyes. Maybe he could see how uncomfortable this whole thing was for me, and he thought my discomfort was fun.

He was a psycho.

I still had no idea why he'd asked me to be his wife. He could've had any woman. With a face like his and his popularity and money, I was sure there'd be women more than willing to be his wife.

So why me?

Did he not want to marry someone he cared about? Someone he liked?

Or did he simply not care about anyone?

But still, why me?

Was it because I didn't have a family? Because it was so easy to whisk me away? Because no one would wonder how I'd ended up with him?

"We've gathered here to—" the man started.

"Yes, we know," Oliver said, waving his hand. "We're not doing that this time. Save it for the big event."

"Yes, sir."

"Skip to the good part."

"You may kiss the bride," the man said.

A little gasp escaped my throat when Oliver grasped my chin, pulling me to him, his lips hovering over mine.

"You can't flinch when I kiss you. People will think I kidnapped you."

"You did." I stared deep into his eyes.

"But you're here of your own free will, are you not?"

I signed the damn deal, so yeah, I was.

Kind of.

Maybe I should've taken a risk and just waited for Oliver to come up with some other favor to ask.

"Have you changed your mind?" His eyes searched mine.

"No."

His lips crashed against mine, intent on devouring me. His kiss was hard and forceful, and strange warmth spread through my body.

When he let go of me, I gasped for breath.

He offered me his arm, and I clung to him as we turned to face the empty room.

"Don't forget to smile as widely as possible," he said.

Smile.

Smile.

And smile.

After this shit was done, I had a feeling like I wasn't going to want to smile ever again.

But my lips were still tingling from his kiss, and I had no idea what to think about that.

"We're going to dance together," he said as he led me to the empty space between the tables.

"Music!" someone shouted.

A slow song started playing, and Oliver wound his arms around me. I placed my hands around his neck.

Too close.

Our faces and our bodies were too close.

When his hands lowered down my back, I looked up into his eyes.

He kept smiling at me, and I smiled back, but it was impossible not to be distracted by his hands that rested on the small of my back.

It was too hot.

The room was too hot.

"Are we done?" I pulled away from him, needing some air.

"Almost." He caught my hand, yanking me to him, and then he dipped me toward the floor.

His hand glided down my stomach as his eyes bored into mine.

My breath got stuck in my chest, and when he pulled me back against his chest, I was slightly lightheaded.

What the hell was he doing to me?

I ripped myself out of his embrace.

I could hear him laugh softly as I strode away from him.

He was enjoying the whole thing a little too much.

Maybe I should've told him I'd changed my mind and watch his reaction, but Matt hadn't been so afraid of him without a good reason.

Oliver was dangerous.

I should never forget that.

CHAPTER TEN

PICKING NEREA TO BE my pretend wife had been the best decision ever. The ceremony had gone even better than expected, and she was breathtaking in her wedding dress.

All eyes were on her.

Mine too.

When she got up from our table and headed toward the terrace, she still had that wonderful smile on her face. Even if it was fake, it didn't matter.

She was so beautiful and seemed so sweet and innocent.

Too good to be true, but exactly what I needed to gain everyone's favor. If they believed a woman as good as she was had chosen me, then I couldn't be the bad guy here.

A dark-haired man with dark eyes slipped out onto the terrace after Nerea. I immediately got to my feet and followed them.

I recognized the man from the photo that Romano had shown me.

It was Clive Willis.

The last person who should be chasing after my wife.

I quickened my steps as I could hear voices coming from the terrace, which wasn't good.

"What does he have on you?" I heard Clive's voice loud and clear. "If you tell me, I can help you."

"I don't know what you're talking about. Oliver and I are—" Nerea said.

"Mr. Willis," I said as I strode toward them, clenching my fists. "We agreed there'd be no interviews tonight. You should leave."

"Ah, Mr. Gavellini. Congratulations! I wasn't trying

to do an interview," Clive said. "I was simply talking to your wife. I didn't know I wasn't supposed to speak with anyone here at all. Is that really such a problem for you?"

"My wife and I don't want our special day ruined." I snaked my arm around Nerea's waist, anger coursing through my veins. "The only reason we let any reporters in tonight was because they all promised not to get in anyone's way. I recall you made the same promise."

"My apologies," Clive said with a smile on his face. "I didn't mean to make your wife or you uncomfortable. I'll go now." His gaze turned to Nerea. "It was nice meeting you."

"You too," Nerea said with a small smile.

Once Clive was gone and we were alone, I caught Nerea's arm.

"Why the fuck did you talk to him?"

She backed away from me, colliding with the wall. "I was just trying to be nice."

"What did you tell him?" I had her trapped between my body and the wall.

"Nothing. I swear." She glared at me.

"You're not allowed to talk to anyone without my permission."

"That's going to make things a bit awkward, won't it? Who is going to believe I'm your wife and not your prisoner if I have to wait for you whenever someone asks me a question?" She lifted her chin up.

"You can talk to the guests, but not to any reporters. Don't forget the terms of our deal."

"I won't." She pressed her lips into a tight line, her chest heaving.

I wanted to kiss her.

I wanted to rip the damn dress off her and bury myself deep inside her.

Right here, right now.

I couldn't remember when the last time I'd wanted something so much was.

And all because of her.

It wasn't like me to lose my mind because of a woman. She'd somehow turned my anger into something else.

I didn't like that.

"Go back inside." I stepped away from her.

She was still looking at me with all the defiance in the world, but she pushed herself off the wall and stormed off.

I turned around and leaned on the railing, gripping it tightly, and stared into the dark night.

Fuck!

CHAPTER ELEVEN

Nerea

I STARED AT THE CEILING as I lay in my bed.

Oliver and I were married now. He'd gotten what he needed.

Or at least I thought he had.

How was I supposed to know if everyone was talking

about our wedding if I didn't even have access to the news?

What did Oliver expect me to do now? Just sit in my room all day and do nothing?

I should ask him.

Getting to my feet, I stormed out of my room, intent on finding him.

When I spotted him—through an open door—sitting on the sofa with a book in his hand, I entered the room.

"I'm not your property," I said to him. "I want to go out, and I want a phone with an internet connection."

His gaze lifted to me, regarding me for a few moments.

He lowered his book and got to his feet.

"Why? So you can talk to that reporter some more?" He cocked his head at me.

"I won't talk to anyone. Why would I? But I'm not your prisoner."

"You're mine for five years. That's what we agreed."

"Yeah, but it didn't say anywhere that I would be trapped in your house for five years with nothing to do! You can't do this to me." I narrowed my eyes at him.

He stepped closer, the corners of his lips tilting up. "It could be worse, you know. I could give you something to do." His voice lowered to a whisper as he leaned in. "I could bend you over the sofa, rip off your panties, and fuck you senseless. I could spill my seed inside you and have you raise my heirs. Would you prefer that?"

My insides clenched with something that wasn't exactly fear as I pictured what he'd just said. Heat shot through my body.

Something was terribly, terribly wrong with me.

"You're disgusting," I said, ignoring the strange sensations low in my stomach.

He shrugged. "I am who I am."

"So you want me to go insane in here."

"You're not locked up in your room. You have the whole house at your disposal. There are plenty of things you can do." He turned away from me and picked up his book. "I have a library on the second floor."

I opened my mouth to argue, but I sensed someone behind my back. When I looked over my shoulder, I saw an armed man in the doorway.

Why had I ever thought that it would be a good idea to play along with a criminal's plan? After all, a criminal was part of the reason why my parents were no longer with me, so why had I expected any decency from Oliver?

He was a jerk who only cared about himself and not about the people whose lives he ruined.

I should've refused his offer and tried to disappear,

and if he had killed me, maybe it would've been better. At least I'd be with my family now.

"Is there anything else you wanted to talk about?" Oliver asked.

Of course there was, but I was too angry, and the armed guy standing behind me didn't help to make me feel any better.

"I guess not," I spat out and strode to the door.

Oliver

EVERY MORNING I GOT up early so I could start working as soon as possible, but today, I just lay in bed and stared at the ceiling because my mind kept going to Nerea.

She'd been so mad at me yesterday, but she also wasn't indifferent to any of what I'd said to her.

There had been a sparkle of need in her eyes. A tiny hitch in her breathing. Her cheeks had flushed.

I shouldn't have even noticed any of that, but for some reason, she intrigued me.

Intrigued me too much.

I had to find a way to end that.

No woman was ever going to get in the way of my goal.

Not even Nerea.

I pushed myself to my feet.

There was work to be done.

"WHAT DID YOU FIND OUT?" I asked.

Romano stood in front of me with a serious expression on his face.

A moment later, he handed me a photo.

I took a quick look at it. Clive was in it with a man I didn't recognize.

"Who's the other guy?" I asked.

"Steve Zayne."

I raised an eyebrow at him because the name didn't ring any bells.

"He's a CIA agent."

"What? Are you sure?"

"Yes."

"What is Clive doing with Zayne? Is he CIA too?"

"I don't know. It isn't easy to get to Clive. But it looks like he has friends in high places. We should be careful about this."

"Are they investigating me?"

"I'm trying to find out, but for now, I don't think it's a good idea to do anything about the reporter. We need to be careful."

I clenched my jaw. That wasn't the kind of news I'd been expecting. I'd rather kill Clive and forget all about him.

"Did Clive report anything about my wedding?" I asked.

"He did, but he only wrote that there's not much the world knows about your mysterious bride. He also implied that she might be living in a golden cage."

I rolled my eyes. "What about the others? What about the Catrona deal? Are they still eating out of Vitrianni's hand?"

"There are some board members who are now more

inclined to give you the deal. They believe you were only trying to protect your wife from the media, and they think you're the best husband in the whole world."

An image of Nerea's furious face flashed in my mind, and I laughed.

They couldn't be more wrong about that. I was a lot of things, but not husband material.

"The plan is working then. That's good," I said.

"Maybe we won't have to worry about Clive anymore if he doesn't find something else to use against you. We still don't know why he's targeting you."

"Look into it. Make sure there are no mistakes because they could cost us."

"I will."

"Is my wife up yet? I'd like to have breakfast with her." Once I saw there was nothing interesting about her or if she annoyed me too much, I could get her out of my head.

Romano's eyebrows shot up. "I don't know, but I'll go check."

"All right."

Romano glanced at me before leaving, unable to hide his surprise.

I always ate breakfast on my own and didn't want to be disturbed, but today, things were different.

When Romano returned, his brow was furrowed. "Um, she's awake, but she refuses to come."

I chuckled. "Then I'll go to her. Set everything up in her room."

"I don't know if that's—"

"That was an order."

Romano inclined his head and hurried out.

I took my phone and attended to some business before heading out into the hallway.

When I entered Nerea's room, everything was already set up, and the food was on the small table the staff had brought in.

Nerea wasn't anywhere in sight, but the bathroom door was closed.

I sat down on the bed.

The bathroom door opened, and Nerea walked out in a purple silk nightgown.

My lips parted, all my blood rushing down to my cock.

It wasn't easy to tear my gaze off her long legs or her breasts.

"What are you doing here?" she snapped.

"I want to have breakfast with you."

"What if I don't want to have breakfast with you?" She pressed her lips into a tight line.

"Aren't you hungry?"

Her stomach rumbled, and her mouth tightened even more.

She strode to the table and snatched a croissant. Then she marched all the way to the other end of the room and leaned against the windowsill, glaring at me as she took a bite.

"That reporter you talked to... His name is Clive Willis, and he's a problem," I said as I took one of the plates.

"You're going to get crumbs all over my bed," Nerea said.

"So? Someone will clean it up."

She rolled her eyes.

"Tell me something about yourself," I said. "Is there anything Clive might try to use against me?"

"I'm sure you already know everything about me." Her gaze was hard on mine.

"Tell me anyway."

"You don't have to worry about Clive finding out anything about my family. They're all dead. I have some relatives who don't live here and that I've never met."

"Your parents died in a house fire, right?"

"Yeah. The firefighters only managed to save me because my bed was in another room." She looked away, her eyes filling with sadness.

"Do you have an ex who might want to try to cash in on some juicy story from your past?" My men hadn't been able to figure any of that out, because if Nerea had ever had a boyfriend, it hadn't been recently.

"I have an ex, but I'm sure he doesn't even remember me by now."

My eyebrows shot up.

Forgetting someone like Nerea?

Unless the guy had amnesia, that sounded impossible.

"What happened with your ex?"

"Why do you care?" She gave me a questioning look.

"I told you. I don't want any surprises with that reporter." That wasn't entirely true because a part of me wanted to know.

It was pure curiosity.

Nothing else.

"Our relationship lasted about four months. Then he got a great job offer in a different town, and he decided that he didn't want to miss the opportunity, so he left."

"And you haven't dated anyone else?"

She shook her head. "What's the point? One way or another, everyone leaves. I focused on work, and I was hoping I'd find a better job eventually. I wasn't looking for a relationship."

She wasn't wrong about that.

Investing in business and yourself had benefits.

Investing in relationships was pointless unless you needed something the other person had, and the other way around.

Relationships were business transactions hidden under the guise of love anyway.

My phone buzzed in my pocket, but I ignored it.

"What about your family? I didn't see them at the wedding." She eyed me carefully. "Were any of the people who said they were your relatives real? Or did you hire them to play their part?"

"I hired them. My father retired and left everything to me, so there's no reason for him to come see me anymore. The last time I heard, my mother was in rehab under a fake identity. I have many cousins and uncles, but they don't live here."

Her mouth fell open. "So you never go see your parents?"

"No. Why would I?"

"Um, because they're your parents?"

I frowned. "I don't need them anymore. My mother raised me, and my father made sure I learned everything I needed to know to run our family business. In exchange for what they did for me, they receive a nice sum of money every month and have my protection too."

"You say that as if your family was hired to have you." There was a peculiar expression on her face. A mix of confusion and something else.

"My father needed an heir so he could retire and enjoy the benefits of what he'd created. Everything he worked hard to build would've been destroyed if he didn't have his own blood to continue his legacy and stop his enemies from getting him and taking what's his."

"Okay, but don't your parents love you? Didn't your father build everything so you could have it one day?"

I snorted. "Love? That's a pile of bullshit invented for fools who don't know any better. My father married my mother only for one purpose, and that was because he didn't want to lose everything and have to fight for his life in his old age. When I was old enough to understand, I learned that no one did anything for free. I had to earn my right to take over his business, and I did."

Nerea watched me as if I'd just told her the saddest thing in the whole world, her eyes glassy. I didn't understand that at all.

My phone buzzed again and I glanced at the screen.

How the hell had so much time passed that I hadn't even noticed?

"I have to go." I got to my feet and strode to the door.

Before I left, I glanced at Nerea.

Her brow was furrowed, her eyes trained on me.

I didn't like the look in her eyes at all, especially because I didn't know what it meant.

Nerea

WHEN ONE OF OLIVER'S men told me I should get ready because Oliver and I were supposed to attend some business dinner at some fancy hotel, I realized that maybe this was my chance to get away.

After talking to Oliver and hearing about his weird

family situation, I kind of felt bad for him, but it only made it clearer to me that I couldn't expect him to behave like a normal human being.

He'd been raised to be a mafia boss.

Someone who wouldn't feel a thing before he pulled the trigger.

Someone who'd be ruthless enough to take what he wanted without caring about anyone else.

I couldn't expect someone like him would care about my needs and wants.

Sure, maybe there was a tiny chance he'd honor our deal, but he was also very likely to kill me. Staying with him just didn't seem like an option.

It was too dangerous and risky for me.

If there were going to be plenty of people at the dinner and if Oliver couldn't bring all his guards with him, then maybe I could find an opportunity to slip away from him.

Once I got out of the house, Oliver opened the car door for me.

He looked breathtakingly handsome in his suit, but I couldn't get distracted by his good looks and forget who he really was.

His gaze traveled down my body and lingered on my golden cocktail dress.

Or maybe he was staring at my body and picturing

me naked.

I got in the car and glanced through the back window. Another car was ready, which probably meant there'd be at least two guards with us.

Oliver settled in the back seat next to me, and the car suddenly seemed too small. He kept stealing glances at me, his hand almost brushing mine.

I hoped I could stay clearheaded enough and not let him intimidate me or make me forget about my plan.

Our ride didn't last very long.

Once the car pulled over in front of the entrance, Oliver got out first. He opened my door and offered me his hand, and I took it.

I forced my lips into a smile because I could see the reporters with their cameras just waiting to snap a photo of us.

Oliver had the most charming smile ever on his face as he led me to the entrance while the cameras clicked. Someone tried to ask a question, but Oliver only waved them away.

"What kind of business party is this?" I asked as we entered the lobby that was crawling with people.

"The regular kind. Except, the mayor and a few important politicians got invited too, so it's kind of a big deal," Oliver said as he led me to a brightly lit room full of tables. "Don't worry. All you have to do here is look pretty. No one will expect you to say anything."

"Right." I glanced over my shoulder.

Two guards trailed after us, watching our surroundings like hawks.

For a second, I wondered how the politicians would feel if they knew a mafia boss was with them tonight, but then I realized they might be part of the whole thing too.

Oliver took me to our table and pulled out a chair for me. The ease with which he played his role here was disturbing.

He smiled.

He was nice.

He was kind.

When in reality, he wasn't any of those things.

I sipped on my wine, waiting for my chance. The guards were sitting at the table next to ours. I eyed the people in the room, pretending to be interested in them.

"I need to go to the restroom," I said, getting to my feet.

"Sure. It's down that hallway to the left," Oliver said, pointing his finger in its direction.

I gave him a small smile, but as soon as I took a few steps, one of the guards rose too.

Great.

I couldn't go anywhere alone and unsupervised, could I? And Oliver saw nothing wrong with that.

When I reached the restroom, there were quite a few people coming and going. Maybe I could lose my guard in the crowd.

He remained outside in the hallway, eyeing everyone around him. I went to the sinks, looking at the mirror. In its reflection, I could see the door that was cracked open and my guard just standing there.

A group of women entered the restroom, chatting excitedly about something.

And then I got an idea.

I waited for them, and then tagged along with their little group. There was a chance my guard wouldn't see me.

I tried to hide as best as possible, and the women were so into their conversation that they didn't even notice I was with them.

My gaze landed on an open door that led to another hallway. Glancing behind me and making sure I couldn't see the guard, I slipped away into the hallway.

I looked over my shoulder, but I couldn't see anyone, so I quickened my steps.

Where did this hallway lead and how could I get out before Oliver and his men found me?

I spotted an elevator and a stairway.

I opted for the stairway. As I climbed down, I hoped I could find an exit.

Maybe there was an underground garage that could help me find a way out. Or maybe I could ask someone to give me a ride.

I ended up in a dim hallway. The first door I tried led to a storage room with no windows.

Shit!

There had to be an emergency exit or something here, but this place was huge and I had no idea where I was going.

I slowed down, my heart thudding loudly in my chest.

When I sensed movement behind me, I spun around, but I couldn't see anyone.

My mind was probably just playing tricks on me.

I turned around and gasped.

Oliver stood in front of me, his face serious, his eyes simmering with anger. He was no longer wearing his suit jacket.

"What the fuck are you doing here?" He caught my wrists and slammed me against the wall.

My breath left me as he pinned my wrists above my head with one hand, trapping me with his strong body.

"I was just... I got lost."

"You got lost?" He sneered. "Do you think I'm an idiot?"

I shook my head.

"Do you know there are cameras in almost every corner of this place? What if my enemy accessed the feed and saw you here all alone instead of me, huh?" His face was so close to mine that I could barely think.

His fingers curved around my chin.

"Someone could've hurt you." His grip on my chin tightened as his gaze focused on my lips.

Had he actually been worried about me? Or was it all just an act?

The fury in his eyes was mixed with something else.

Desire.

Need.

I bit down on my lip.

"Nothing happened," I breathed. "I'm fine."

"Yeah, you are." The anger vanished from his eyes, but he didn't let go of me.

Instead, he gently trailed his fingers down my bare arms.

A shiver of delight rushed through me.

He lowered his lips toward mine, his grip on my chin loosening.

Only a breath away.

Instead of turning my head away from him, I just kept looking into the blue depths of his eyes.

My lips moved toward his.

I couldn't deny that his touch always woke up something inside me, but I'd never wanted to think about it too much before.

I'd kissed him before, or well, he'd kissed me.

But it had been for show.

And now...

I pressed my lips against his, not even sure why.

Maybe it was just curiosity.

Maybe I wanted to know if the flames inside me would burst into something stronger.

Oliver's body tensed, but then he kissed me back, his tongue pushing past my lips.

Fire roared inside my veins, coming to life stronger than ever, as Oliver pressed himself even tighter against me, his erection poking at me through his pants.

My insides shivered, and I let myself enjoy the sensations as he deepened our kiss.

His hand wound around my throat, and he pushed me back.

I let out a gasp.

My need was still there, stronger than ever, and I didn't know what to do with it.

"Don't do that," he said softly, releasing me. "Don't

do that unless you want me to take you upstairs to my room and fuck your brains out."

I wanted to tell him that would never happen.

I didn't even like him as a person.

But the past few weeks had been so damn stressful, and I wanted something nice.

I wanted to feel good.

I wanted my release, even if it was with him.

"Where is that room?" I said, my voice hoarse.

His eyes widened in surprise for a fraction of a second, but then he brought his lips to mine again until I was gasping for breath.

He tugged me with him to an elevator, and as we were on our way up, he wound his arms around me, his lips hard on mine.

I had no idea how we'd made it to a room or if anyone had seen us, but as soon as Oliver opened the door, he yanked me inside.

He had me against the wall again, his hands roaming my body and tugging at my dress. I tilted my head as he left a path of kisses down my neck, his hand cupping my breast and squeezing.

A soft moan escaped my lips when he unzipped my dress and yanked it down my body.

He lifted me up then and carried me to the bed. I held onto him as he kept kissing me.

When he lowered me onto the bed, he ripped his shirt off him and tossed it away. He climbed on top of me, and I ran my hand down his strong, muscular chest.

He tugged on my bra so hard that the clasp broke. I let out a gasp as he exposed my breasts and lowered his head, taking my nipple into his mouth.

His hand traveled down my stomach as he sucked on my hard bud, sending hundreds of wonderful sensations through me.

His hand slipped into my panties, his fingers rubbing my wetness. I groaned as his tongue trailed around my nipple, his teeth grazing me, while his fingers kept playing with my pussy.

He lowered his mouth down my stomach, yanking my panties down my legs. When he looked up at me, I spread my legs wide for him.

He buried his head between my thighs, his tongue darting out. My insides tingled with pleasure as his tongue parted my folds.

When his tongue found my clit, teasing and probing, I curled my fingers in the sheets, unable to stay still.

All the wonderful things Oliver was doing with his tongue set my body even more on fire, and when two of his fingers pushed inside my opening, I let out a loud moan.

His fingers and his tongue hit all the right spots, spilling me over the edge.

I tried to catch my breath as he pushed himself up and started unbuttoning his pants. When he pulled down his underwear, the sight of his thick length sent another rush of arousal through me.

He grabbed a condom from the nightstand drawer. When he moved on top of me again, positioning himself between my legs. I was like a bubble of need ready to burst.

Oliver rubbed himself against me, and I groaned. And then he pushed himself deep into my wetness, making me take him all in as I stretched around him.

His lips found mine as he pumped into me, his thrusts hard and fast. I wrapped my arms around him as he rammed himself inside me again and again.

I pushed my hips against his, letting the pleasure overtake me.

Oliver's body moved against mine as he pounded into me, and when I couldn't take it any longer, my orgasm spread through me like a wave, making it impossible to think about anything else.

There was just pure bliss.

I cried out, and Oliver grunted, his release joining mine.

His mouth brushed mine before he pulled away from me.

But even though my body felt as if it were floating on a cloud of ecstasy, I couldn't help but wonder what the hell I had just done and why it had felt so damn good and right.

WHEN I OPENED MY EYES, the first thing I saw was Nerea's face.

It was disconcerting for a moment because I'd never woken up next to someone before. Whenever I fucked someone, I'd be out as soon as possible.

Nerea was still asleep, looking as beautiful as ever. Her face was peaceful, with no trace of anger or worry.

A smile started to spread across my lips, but I stopped myself in time.

What the fuck was I doing?

I'd had her, and now my strange interest in her should be over.

But it wasn't, and I wouldn't mind being inside her again.

With a groan, I pushed myself up and grabbed my phone. My eyes widened when I saw the time.

It was fucking late.

I usually never needed an alarm because I'd wake up for work all on my own, but today...

Nerea was seriously messing with my brain for some reason.

She shifted, shoving the covers off her and giving me a nice view of her bare thighs. My cock twitched.

Fuck.

I could claim her over and over again, and I didn't think it would be enough.

But I had things to do.

My inbox was full of messages.

Romano wanted to talk to me about something urgent, so I reluctantly got out of bed, leaving Nerea alone.

After a quick, cold shower that didn't help me clear my head at all, I got dressed and slipped out of the room.

Romano waited for me in the lobby.

Nerea and I shouldn't have stayed at the hotel, but I had no regrets about that.

"Let's go outside," I said to Romano because I didn't want to risk someone overhearing us.

Once we were far enough away, I turned to him.

"Our shipment is on its way," Romano said, and I knew what he was talking about. "A fruit truck is bringing it to us. Should be here by midnight."

"All right. Keep me updated." I trusted my men could handle today's cocaine shipment just fine without needing my help.

"I will. There shouldn't be any trouble. I have some men checking out the roads to make sure there aren't any surprises."

"Good."

"There's something else. It's about your wife."

"What about her?" I eyed him carefully.

"Everyone seems to like her. The press is constantly calling and asking for interviews with her."

"Tell them Nerea and I want our privacy respected. There's no reason for them to want to speak with her."

"People are curious about her because she managed to capture the heart of one of the most wanted bachelors. They want to know more about how it happened. They want to know what's so special about her. And some would like to do a photo shoot with her because she's pretty."

"Reject all of it."

"It might not be a bad idea to let her do an interview or a photo shoot."

"Why?" I narrowed my gaze at him.

"I was told that Clive is writing another article, and it might not be good for you."

"Who cares what he writes about? We've done everything to convince people that Nerea and I are in love. What else is there to say?"

"Apparently, Clive is worried that she's never out on her own. He thinks that it's odd that a young, now rich, girl like her doesn't go out on shopping sprees and doesn't hang out with her friends. He's going to point out that she didn't even have a bachelorette party and that she has no friends or family. He's probably going to try to make it sound like you're using Nerea simply because she was poor and had no one to protect her from you."

I ground my teeth together because that wasn't all that far from the truth.

"So what if she was on her own? She's only five years younger than me, and I didn't have a bachelor party either. Why isn't he talking about that? Why does he think he has to know everything?"

"It's possible someone else is behind all this and has a reason to push this story. Clive might only be a puppet. Someone might be waiting for you to make a mistake. You know how important the Catrona deal is. There might be another player who wants their piece of the cake."

"Then have that fucking investigated! Don't waste both our time just talking to me about it," I snapped.

"I will, but since Nerea and you stayed at the hotel, I thought that maybe now—"

"If you think something changed, forget it. Sex is just sex. She's not going to look at me any different."

"Mmm-hmm."

"What?"

"Nothing."

"Then go." I pulled out my phone so I could order some breakfast for Nerea and me, and headed back.

By the time I reached the room that was always reserved for me in case I needed it, like last night, Nerea had just opened the door to let the staff with our breakfast in.

When they were gone, she sat on the bed and watched me carefully. She had a white robe on, but even in it, she looked absolutely gorgeous.

I grabbed a piece of toast and settled on the bed next to her. She took a plate and filled it with food.

"Do you already know what you're going to do when our five years are up?" I asked because the silence was getting unbearable.

"I guess. Before my grandma passed, she made me promise I'd find our relatives in Spain because she'd lost contact with them after she moved away with my grandpa. She made some things for them—jewelry and sweaters—and she had some photos and family heirlooms she wanted them to have. She was sure her older sister had children and probably even grandchildren that I could find. I always hoped I could save enough money to fulfill her wish. It was actually my only goal, aside from trying to find a better job."

"You don't want anything else?"

"Not really. We never know what will happen, so why plan anything if our plans will be ruined?"

"Why would they be ruined?" I frowned.

"Because of fate." She sighed.

"Fate?" I arched my eyebrows. "We make our own fate."

"We try, but in the end..." She shook her head. "Forget it. I guess *you* don't expect fate will get in your way."

"I don't. If something stops me from reaching my

goal of ruling this city, it will be my own fault. No one and nothing else's."

"Is ruling the city the only thing you want?" She tilted her head.

"No, but it's the most important one. I want to be one of the richest men in the country and expand my family's empire."

"Are you talking about crime here or about something else? You have a legit business too, right?"

"Of course I do. You need both to make things work."

"Why would you need both? Why not just run your legit business and become rich by being a good person?"

I laughed. "Do you know anyone who got rich and powerful by being a good person? Things don't work that way. You can try to be good, but then someone who's not will take what's yours. Many times, you have to play dirty."

"And is it worth it? You'll end up as the most powerful man out there, and then what? Who cares? Will it make you happy? Will you have someone to share it with? Or will you just swim in a pool of dollar bills all on your own? Are you going to save the world? Feed the poor? Tell me, what's the point of your big goal?"

"You don't know what you're talking about." I furrowed my brow.

Nerea

"MAYBE YOU'RE RIGHT. I never wanted to be a mafia boss, so what do I know?" I popped a piece of toast in my mouth. "Do you ever think about the people who suffer because of what you do?"

"Do you think anyone out there would care if *I*

suffered? Why should I give a fuck about anyone else when everyone's always only looking out for themselves? And most people know exactly what they're getting themselves into."

I narrowed my eyes at him. "So you think it's okay to kill some guy's whole family because he betrayed you or because he's your enemy?"

"It's how things work. The guy is the one who put his family at risk. If anything happens to them because of him, it's his fault." His face was serious.

"But they're innocent in the whole thing!"

"They might be, but he's not."

"What about the people who suffer because people like you take away their jobs? What about the people who died because they found themselves in the mafia's path by accident? What about the people who are forced to work for you because they have no choice? What about all the people—"

"Everyone has a choice. You can think some greater force is punishing you, or you can take matters into your own hands and find a way to get what you want. You can join your enemy, you can run away, you can fight... There are plenty of options."

"What if that choice isn't fair?"

"Life isn't fair either. So what?"

"What would've happened if you refused to take over after your father? Did you have a choice?"

His frown deepened. "I never thought about refusing. Not even for a second. I wanted to succeed."

"But could you have changed your mind and just left?"

He was quiet for a few moments. "My father would've hunted me down and killed me. It would've been a risk for him to leave me alive."

"And you think that's okay?"

He nodded.

"But you didn't choose to be born into a mafia family."

"I didn't, but I could've chosen to leave. If I got caught and killed, it would be my own fault. Everything we do has consequences."

"That's messed up. I don't even like the idea of a world where it's okay for a father to kill his son just because his son doesn't want to follow in his footsteps."

"When you invest everything in that son, and instead of paying you back, he leaves and holds the power to destroy you in his hands, you have to do something about it before he talks to the wrong people."

"Or you can be a good father and just love your son and let him live in peace! Who even says he's going to try to destroy you?"

"What do you get in exchange if you do that?" he asked.

"Um, why would you have to get anything in exchange?"

"If you don't, you have just wasted your time and money. It's a bad investment."

"Children aren't investments."

"Yes, they are. You either expect to get something out of them in the future, or you have them because they give you a certain kind of feeling that you want to experience."

"If your father saw you as an investment, then what about your mother?"

"She had me because that was what my father expected of her in exchange for everything he provided for her."

"You said she ended up in rehab."

He gave me a nod. "She was only eighteen when she married my father and had me. I guess she expected her life would be amazing, and she did get what she wanted, but she also got hooked on drugs because it was all too much for her. The life with my father and me wasn't what she'd been hoping for. She thought it would be easier."

"But she took care of you, right?"

"Only while I was very young. I don't remember any

of it. My father sent me to his brother's private school when I was four."

"What kind of private school?" I could barely believe that Oliver was telling me all this.

Maybe I should just tell him to stop before I found out too much and he decided that I was a threat when I was no longer useful to him, but I wanted to understand him.

I wanted to know why he was the way he was.

I wanted to know why the concept of love was so foreign to him.

"My family is actually very big. My grandfather had thirteen children. Most of them stayed in Italy to run the business, but my father moved here and built almost everything all on his own. His brothers had many children too, so one of my uncles decided to open a private school for all the kids. He thought that people like us needed a different kind of education that we wouldn't receive in a regular school. He had to pull a few strings to get the school approved, and then all the kids attended it under fake names so that no one would realize it belonged just to one family. We lived there and learned everything we needed."

"You never attended a regular school?"

He shook his head. "There was no need for that. We had more important things to do and learn. Once I was done with school, it was easier for my father to show me the ropes of our own business here."

"More important things? Like what? Killing people?"

"It's a useful skill when everyone's out there to kill you because of who you are."

"When was the first time you killed someone?"

"When I was six."

I gaped at him. "How?"

"My uncle brought some prisoners. People who stole from him. They were tied up and blindfolded. Those of us who were chosen had to cut their throats. It's also how we paid for school, by doing things for our uncle."

"But you were just a child."

"And if I hadn't learned how to defend myself and kill, I would've died when I was fourteen and an enemy attacked me."

"Was there anything nice about your uncle's school? Anything fun?" I didn't really want to know all the gruesome details.

"Yeah. I loved it when I had to get creative to steal food. It wasn't as fun if I got caught, but it was easier to steal than to earn it because the tasks tended to be complicated."

I blinked at him. "You had to do things for food?"

"Yeah, of course. The easiest thing to do was clean the school, but it was also the most boring one. I got a pizza once all for myself because I successfully spied on an enemy and brought some very important information to my uncle."

He was actually smiling.

As if those were his super happy memories.

Oh hell.

No one had ever been there for him when he needed it, and he'd spent his childhood in some crazy mafia school.

Tears filled the corners of my eyes, but I pushed them back.

"What's wrong?" he asked, confusion written all over his face.

"Does your uncle's school still exist?"

"Yeah."

"Do you plan on sending your children there one day?"

"No. I don't care what happens after I die, so I don't want any. I'm not like my father. I'll never retire. They'll have to kill me first. And when I'm dead, I won't care if it all goes to hell. One of my cousins can take over, or they can fight it out. But I don't plan on dying anytime soon."

I grabbed a bottle of water and took a big gulp. Oliver didn't even realize how wrong what had happened to him was. I doubted he'd even thought about it.

Now I wasn't surprised at all that his views about things were so twisted.

Was he ever going to realize his family had deprived him of the most basic things that every child needed?

My parents might have died, but my grandparents had made sure I'd had all the safety, love, and support that I'd needed.

Oliver hadn't had any of that.

Would he get it one day?

Or would it be too late?

CHAPTER SIXTEEN

Oliver

I TRIED TO FOCUS ON work and start a new project, but my mind kept going back to Nerea and our conversation.

Why the fuck had I told her all that stuff about me and my uncle's school? How was I going to let her go in five years if she knew all that?

And that look in her eyes...

She'd been horrified and sad, and I had no idea why.

Why did she even ask me anything and pretend she cared?

Except, it hadn't looked like she'd been pretending.

A knock sounded on the door, yanking me out of my thoughts.

"Come in," I said.

Romano entered the room. "Clive is going to publish his article tomorrow. He claims you're not letting Nerea out of your sight, and that she's not allowed to go anywhere on her own."

"What am I supposed to do with those ridiculous claims?"

"Send Nerea out with the guards. She can go shopping, or we can have some girl grab a coffee with her. I don't think Clive will know if the girl is a friend or not. Even if he claims it's all fake, I doubt many will believe him with actual proof showing otherwise, especially if you do this before the article goes live."

I'd had it with Clive and his stupid articles.

"Fuck it. I'll take Nerea out, and I don't give a shit about that asshole," I said.

"But—"

"No."

"Should I let some reporters know where you'll be going so that they can take photos?"

"No."

I had no idea what Clive was up to, but if he thought he could rattle me or get in my way with some stupid articles and his CIA friend, he was wrong.

"WHERE ARE WE GOING?" Nerea asked as I drove the car deeper and deeper into the woods.

"You'll see."

She clasped her hands on her lap, wringing her fingers, and kept glancing outside.

Maybe she was wondering where the guards were. I'd ordered them not to follow us. Nerea and I would be safe here because no one knew or expected I'd go in this direction.

It wasn't a very popular or busy area. My men would alert me if anyone suspicious headed this way.

I swerved off the road and followed a narrow path. When I pulled over, Nerea eyed me with suspicion.

"Relax," I said. "I didn't bring you all the way here to kill you."

Her lips didn't even twitch.

Shit.

Did she think I was going to kill her?

If I were in her place, I'd probably believe the same, but I had no intention of hurting her.

At least not today.

"Come," I said when we got out of the car.

I'd been here a lot, so it was easy to recognize the trees and find the right path that led to the river.

Nerea looked around in wonder.

Everywhere around us, birds chirped, the leaves rustled, and the water splashed against rocks.

"Do you like it?" I asked.

She nodded. "Do you come here often?"

"Yeah, when I want to get away from everything and when I need to clear my head." I pulled my shirt over my head and kicked off my shoes.

Nerea's eyes widened, and a spark of desire flashed through them as I pulled my pants down.

"Wanna join me?" I glanced over my shoulder at her as I headed toward the river.

"Is it cold?" she asked.

"Come and find out." I threw myself in the river.

When I looked toward Nerea, she was taking off her shirt.

A smile spread across my lips when she tiptoed toward the river in her underwear. She hesitated as she just stood there.

I waved her over.

Finally, she got in.

"It's freezing!" She wrapped her arms around herself. "Are you crazy?"

"It's not." I got closer to her and pulled her into my embrace. "Better now?"

"Yeah." She let out a laugh.

She pressed herself close to me, clinging to me.

Her eyes met mine.

"Is this your favorite secret place or something?" she asked.

I nodded.

"Why did you bring *me* here then?"

It was a good question, and I didn't know the answer.

I usually didn't want to share this place with anyone.

I'd always wanted to be alone.

Romano knew about it, just in case something happened, but I'd never let him or anyone follow me all the way here.

Instead of answering, I kissed her.

Her mouth responded to mine without hesitation.

With her here, I liked this place even better.

"Okay, I'm getting out now." She shivered as she pulled away from me. "It's nice, but I'd rather be out there in the sun."

"Okay." I grinned.

But once she got out, I realized my mistake.

She realized it too.

My gun was right there with my clothes. What the fuck was wrong with me?

It was the stupidest thing I'd ever done. Something that hadn't happened to me ever since I'd misplaced my gun at my uncle's school and nearly gotten shot as punishment.

I hadn't been thinking that Nerea might get her hands on it at all.

She eyed the gun, but then she sat down on the grass.

Why hadn't she at least tried to pick it up?

So what if she didn't know how to shoot?

Even if she didn't want to kill me, she could've run away, so why hadn't she?

I headed toward her.

"Did you bring any food?" she asked when I reached her. "I'm starving."

"I'll have someone bring something. Whatever you

want." It would mean that my men would get to see this place too, but it was my fault for forgetting to bring some food, and I'd only let my most trusted ones come here, so it wasn't a big deal.

All I wanted was to stay here with Nerea for a while longer.

CHAPTER SEVENTEEN

Nerea

WHEN OLIVER'S MEN BROUGHT us food, I dug in. Oliver hadn't let them get too close to us, and he'd sent them away immediately.

I had no idea why he was doing this, but it was really

nice. It was great to be away from everyone and everything.

Just us and nature.

Maybe I'd been wrong about Oliver.

Maybe there was still hope for him.

Just because he kept people away from him because he thought everyone wanted something from him and that he should treat every relationship like a business transaction didn't mean that deep down he was a bad person.

Okay, now I was hallucinating.

Oliver was a mafia boss, so of course he wasn't an angel, but maybe he wasn't completely bad.

Maybe if he got a chance to see that there were things in life other than money and power that were worth fighting for, then he might change his mind about everything.

But who was I to tell him anything about that?

I didn't want to get too attached to people because, in the end, I always ended up alone. Even my deal with Oliver had an expiration date, just like everything else.

Maybe I should've taken his gun, even if I had no clue what to do with it since I'd never even held one before. I could've threatened him or tried to shoot him.

I could've been free.

But we were in the middle of nowhere, and I didn't

think I had it in me to kill Oliver, so he would've found me anyway.

And then he would've killed me for sure.

I cleaned my hands with a wet wipe and settled next to Oliver again.

As he pressed himself closer to me while we lay on a blanket his men had brought with the food too, I suddenly thought of something else.

What if he was doing this for a reason?

Were reporters going to jump out of some bush and take photos of us?

Was that why we were here?

It would be the perfect setup. Just the two of us, trying to enjoy a romantic outing, and Oliver hadn't told me anything about it because he wanted me to appear natural.

"What?" Oliver asked as I kept glancing around.

"Nothing."

"Don't lie to me." He placed his hand on my cheek, caressing.

"I just want to be sure that we're really alone here."

"We are." He leaned closer and captured my lips with his.

Warmth instantly shot through me.

Why was it so easy for him to light a fire inside me?

I kissed him back, my hand trailing down his stomach.

He groaned as my fingers brushed his cock through his underwear.

I had no idea if he was telling me the truth, but I felt brave.

Slipping my hand into his underwear, I cupped him and stroked him as he grew hard under my touch.

He shifted and slid his fingers under the waistband of my panties.

I let out a sound low in my throat as he started rubbing me.

I kept running my fingers over his length as he pressed his finger over my clit.

His eyes met mine as we stroked each other.

Pleasure raced through my body, and I couldn't look away from him.

Our releases hit us almost at the same time, and we both let out a cry.

We lay back, gasping for breath.

When our gazes connected again, Oliver smiled at me, and I smiled too.

It would be easy to pretend that he was someone else.

Here, we were just two people.

Free.

Without any of the burdens that weighed on us.

If only this moment could last forever.

But everything always came to an end, and this would too.

All I could do was enjoy it while it lasted.

CHAPTER EIGHTEEN

Oliver

"IT WOULDN'T BE A BAD idea if you stopped on your way home and went for a walk in the park for a bit," Romano said. "I know you don't care about the reporters, but I know you care about that deal."

"Fine. I'll take Nerea for a walk before going back." I ended the call with a sigh.

"What's going on?" Nerea asked.

We were on the road again, but instead of heading back home, there was a change of plans.

But if I had to go for a walk with Nerea because of the reporters, I'd rather do it now when we were both relaxed.

"It looks like we're not free from reporters. We'll have to take a walk in the city for everyone to see. And then I'll sue Clive for his baseless claims and attempts to damage my reputation. I don't care who he is or who he really works for."

"Oh, okay."

"But first we need to switch to a different car and get the guards. Unless you'd prefer to do something else." I glanced at her.

"No, it's fine. Actually, I'd like to go for a walk. I miss the city."

I'd had her trapped in my house and my world too much. Some normalcy—or some resemblance of it—would do her good.

"I LOVE THIS PARK," Nerea said, holding onto my arm. "I used to come here with my grandma all the time. Well, back when she could still walk. I miss her so much."

"Is there anything else you miss?" I asked.

Her face was pensive for a few moments. "Oh! There was this awesome ice cream place just around the corner. I don't know if it still exists."

"Let's check."

Her lips spread into a smile, and it was so beautiful and genuine.

Where were those damn reporters now?

I hadn't seen a single one.

Nerea led me down an alley. Just as we were about to round the corner, I spotted a shadow out of the corner of my eye.

I pushed Nerea to the ground, shielding her, as I pulled out my gun. The guards had their guns out too, just as the attacker fired at us.

I caught Nerea's arm and tugged her with me as I

fired at the attackers that kept coming and jumping out of their hiding spots.

"Stay here," I said to Nerea as she crouched behind a dumpster at the end of the alley.

Her eyes were wide, her face pale, but she bobbed her head.

She'd be fine.

I gritted my teeth when I saw one of my guards jerk back as a bullet caught him in the side.

Rushing out toward him, I pulled the trigger and forced my enemy to duck.

Something was wrong here.

We'd been expecting reporters, not an attack.

I had a feeling this had been planned, and someone had just waited for us to show up so they could attack.

One of the reporters had to be working with my enemy.

These guys might be Vitrianni's.

But there was no time to think about that.

We had to end this fight sooner rather than later because we couldn't let actual reporters take photos of any of this or have the cops arrive too quickly and find us.

I pressed myself against the wall, taking a peek around the corner.

Once one of the attackers was in sight, I fired at him and hit him in the head.

The guy fell to the ground.

I used the opportunity to race to the other side to check on my guard, who was lying on the ground with a hand over his stomach.

His fingers were coated in blood.

"You need to get out of here, sir," he choked out. "If someone—"

"Don't speak. Everything's going to be fine." I crouched next to him and quickly texted for backup, along with sending our coordinates.

My other guard was still firing at someone I couldn't see from the spot where I was.

I glanced in the direction of Nerea's hiding place to make sure she wasn't in any danger.

A few moments later, my guard came running.

"Sir!" he yelled. "Three are down. One ran away."

"Did you see who they were?"

He shook his head.

"We need to get out of here. Help me get Ben up."

"Yes, sir."

Ben groaned as we caught him by the arms and lifted him up.

"Leave me," Ben muttered. "I—"

"No, we're not leaving you. Come on."

We moved as fast as we could.

"Nerea!" I yelled. "Come!"

She got to her feet, looking at us with worry in her eyes.

A van sped toward us, and Nerea backed away.

"It's okay," I said.

The van pulled over, and one of my men opened the back. We managed to get Ben inside, and I caught Nerea's hand to pull her with me.

Once we were all in the van, the driver turned toward me.

"Take us to the clinic. Now!" I said.

Ben groaned again.

I spotted a cloth and grabbed it, pressing it against his wound. "Nerea, help him hold it."

She was on the other side of Ben, and she placed her hand over the cloth.

I wiped my bloody fingers on my pants and pulled out my phone so I could call Romano.

"Send a message to our doctor and tell him to get ready. Ben got shot," I said when Romano answered.

"I did that as soon as I found out you called for backup. What happened?"

"Someone was waiting for Nerea and me to show up in a public place. Did you tip off any reporters about where we were going to be?"

"Yeah, a few of them."

"One of them is working with our enemy. Find out who and make them pay." I trusted Romano.

He would never put me in danger.

In fact, he'd risked his life for me more than once.

"I will," he said. "Do you need anything else?"

"Not right now." I ended the call.

When we reached the clinic, the doctor who was on our payroll was already waiting outside with a gurney.

The nurses helped us get Ben out of the van and rushed him inside.

"Do you want me to take you home, sir?" the driver asked.

"Not yet. I'll stay. Call Ben's family."

"Yes, sir."

I turned to Nerea. "If you want to leave—"

"No," she said. "I'll stay too."

"All right. Let's go inside."

We had to be careful.

"Sam," I said to the other guard. "Take a look around and make sure there isn't anyone suspicious lurking close by. If there are any reporters out there, alert me immediately."

"Yes, sir."

When he was gone, Nerea and I took a seat in the chairs that were in the hallway.

"Is that the bathroom over there?" Nerea asked. "I need to wash my hands."

"Yeah."

Some of Ben's blood was on her fingers.

Even though she'd witnessed something that wasn't what she was used to, she'd handled it well.

Nerea was stronger than she even knew.

As I watched her, I wondered if maybe she'd want to stay with me, even after our contract was fulfilled.

But that was a crazy thought.

No one in their right mind would want to stay with me, no matter what I offered in exchange.

Nerea

WHEN I WAS BACK FROM the bathroom, Oliver was talking to a woman and the doctor. I waited until the woman and the doctor left and Oliver was alone.

"Is your guard going to be okay?" I asked.

"Yeah. His wife just came to see him."

I watched him for a long moment. Even though the whole thing about the attack had been scary and shocking, there was something else that had surprised me more.

"Why do you care?" I asked.

"What?" He blinked at me.

"Why are we here?"

His brow furrowed. "I don't know what you're asking."

"Well, you keep saying that no one does anything for free, especially not you. You're paying the guard, right? Getting hurt is part of his job. And yet, you brought him here, and you stayed. I can't help but wonder why."

"Because that man would give his life for me. Making sure he's okay is the least I can do," he said. "I pay people to work for me, but if I want their loyalty, I need to be loyal to them too. They protect me. I protect them. Maybe I won't jump in front of a bullet to save them, but I will do everything in my power to make sure they don't have to die for me."

A small smile spread across my lips.

Now, I believed that there was hope for Oliver more than ever. Maybe his logic was a little twisted and weird at times, and maybe he wasn't quite aware of it, but I was sure he cared about his men.

Like, really cared.

Maybe I could get to know him some more, and I might even decide to stay with him. He might keep his word to me and let me go after five years. Going off on my own now might be extremely dangerous, and not just because Oliver would be after me.

Someone else might come for me too in hopes of getting to Oliver.

I could treat this as a weird vacation or something like that.

Then I'd be free to do whatever I wanted.

But could I trust Oliver with my life?

He'd protected me today, but would he keep doing it?

Or did he just want to use me for sex and company?

I'd never dated or tried to date a mafia boss before, so this whole thing was new to me. I didn't know what to expect.

I didn't know what was normal in a situation like this.

Maybe I was deluding myself and trying to see good where there wasn't any.

There were still so many things I didn't know about him, and there was no way for me to know how or if he even felt something for me.

I supposed he liked me enough to spend time with me and tell me some things about himself, but was that out of pure loneliness? Or could there be something more?

"What are you thinking?" he asked, pulling me out of my thoughts.

"Nothing. I'm just glad we're all okay."

"What happened today wasn't supposed to happen. I'll make sure that you never find yourself in danger like that. I should've taken more precautions and had my men check the area first."

"Do you know who attacked us?"

"Not yet, but I will soon." His face darkened. "And they're going to regret it."

The scary mafia boss was back, but I wasn't afraid of him anymore.

Maybe I should be, but for some reason, I felt like he and I were on the same side and that he wouldn't hurt me.

Only time would tell if I was right.

CHAPTER TWENTY

Oliver

FOR THE PAST FEW DAYS, I'd seen more TV shows than in my whole life.

As soon as I gave Nerea access to my streaming TV service, she'd somehow managed to get me to watch it with her. Apparently, watching TV shows was her favorite pastime.

When I entered the room, her face was glued to the screen, but she looked up at me, and a smile spread across her lips.

"Hurry! You don't want to miss this scene!" She waved me over, and then launched into an explanation about the characters and what was going on.

I didn't even care about what she was saying, but for some reason, I enjoyed listening to her voice. Every time she smiled, it was like the room became brighter.

I offered her the bowl of popcorn I'd brought, and she immediately grabbed it and placed it on her lap.

"Do you think this guy is the killer?" she asked.

"I don't know." I snatched some popcorn from the bowl.

"I think he is. He has that look."

"What look?"

She turned toward me, narrowing her eyes, then shook her head. "Never mind. I keep forgetting you're…"

I chuckled.

"It's so weird," she said. "I know who you are and what you do, and we got shot at, but I somehow still can't completely wrap my head around the whole thing. But forget about that. Do you want to play a video game with me later? I saw you have a nice collection."

"They're Romano's. I never play."

She gaped at me. "You never played a video game? Are you kidding me?"

"No. I don't have any interest in games. It's a waste of time."

"That's a shame. I love to play, and it's always more fun when you play it with someone else. I used to play with random people online."

"I can try. If you want." I had no idea why I'd just said that.

But Nerea liked it.

It would make her happy.

So why not?

"I'd love that!" She grinned. "But I have to warn you. I'm not going to let you win."

I laughed. "You don't have to."

A knock sounded on the door.

"What?" I didn't like that we were being interrupted.

I might be neglecting some of my duties because of this, but it wouldn't be the end of the world. Things could run just fine without me, as long as nothing major happened.

Romano poked his head through the door.

"How important is it?" I asked.

"Very," he said.

I groaned, pushing myself to my feet.

"Do you want me to pause the show and wait for you?" Nerea asked.

"No, you keep watching."

"Okay." She flashed me a smile.

She was really passionate about her TV shows. Who would've thought?

Once Romano and I were in the hallway, I focused my attention on him.

"Those men who attacked you. They're Vitrianni's," he said.

"That's not a surprise." Not many people would be dumb enough to try to go against me, and not many would've been able to sneak through my territory just like that. "I knew I shouldn't listen to you when you said Nerea and I had to be seen in public."

"I'm sorry. I didn't expect—"

"I know. It's not your fault. What about the reporter who tipped off Vitrianni?"

"We found him. He'll no longer be a problem."

"At least some good news. Did anyone take photos or videos of the attack?"

"As far as we know, no. What do you want me to do about Vitrianni? Everyone expects you to retaliate."

I scratched the back of my neck. "Yeah, and that's what I would usually do. But now... I think it might be a trap."

"What kind of trap?"

"You dealt with that reporter, but Clive is still out there, writing his bullshit. Imagine if I attacked Vitrianni and someone recorded the whole thing. Vitrianni's men attacked me and my wife. Since they failed to kill us, it's expected that I'd want to make Vitrianni pay and show him that I'm not a coward like him. Even if they didn't plan that from the beginning, they would do it now."

"We can follow Clive, and then you can attack Vitrianni once we know Clive is too far away to do any damage."

"It wouldn't help, and they could always use a different reporter, or record something themselves and send it to Clive. What I do know is that they won't openly publish the recording to the whole world themselves because no one in their right mind would agree to work with them after such a move. But the whole thing is suspicious. First, Clive wrote his silly articles to get a reaction out of me. He wanted me to take Nerea out, and he expected we'd tip off other reporters about our whereabouts. I wouldn't be surprised if Clive was working with Vitrianni, and that the other reporter was just a decoy."

"But what about Clive's CIA friend?"

"You couldn't find any proof they're friends. There's

just that one photo. It means nothing. And who cares? It wouldn't be the first time someone played both sides."

"What are we going to do then?"

"I'll think of something, but we can't make any rash moves. It would be a mistake."

Vitrianni would get what he deserved, but that didn't have to be now.

I could be patient and wait for the right moment.

Nerea

I SEARCHED FOR OLIVER, but I couldn't find him anywhere. Where the hell was he?

We'd spent a few wonderful weeks together, and it was really nice.

If he had to go somewhere, he would always tell me,

so I didn't think he'd left me alone here now without saying a word to me about it.

When I reached the part of the house I didn't think I'd had the chance to see before since it was way too big, I thought about turning back, but then I heard a noise coming from the end of the hallway.

I inched closer to the sound, and when I reached the door, I stopped.

Oliver was shirtless, and he was punching a bag in what looked like a small gym.

He was alone.

I leaned in the doorway, just watching him.

Or better said, drooling.

Why did he have to be so damn hot? One look at his lean, strong body was enough to start a fire inside me.

A smile spread across his lips, and then he looked up at me.

"Are you spying on me?" he teased.

"Maybe." I entered the room, looking around.

It was full of exercising equipment.

He took off his gloves and tossed them onto a table in the corner of the room. Then he strolled toward me.

"Now that you're here, I could show you one of my favorite activities," he said.

"And what would that be?" I tilted my head at him.

"Hand-to-hand combat."

"Yeah, I don't think I'd be good at that. I never even punched anyone."

"You can try to punch me. If you succeed, I'll give you my laptop with internet access."

My mouth fell open. "Seriously? Why don't we just skip the punching thing, and you just give me your laptop?"

"Nuh-uh. You have to win it." A smile curved his lips.

"Fine." I narrowed my eyes at him.

"Come at me." He spread out his arms.

I awkwardly started toward him, my fist raised.

"You're doing it wrong."

I stopped, looking at my fist. "I'm not even doing anything."

"Wait." He got hold of my arm, his fingers trailing over my skin.

I could barely focus when he was touching me like that.

"Hold it like this." He lifted my arm.

"Okay. Now what?"

He moved behind me, his hands traveling my body and guiding me until I was in the right position.

A shot of electricity surged through me.

"Now punch," he said.

I moved my fist through the air. "Like this?"

"Yeah. Now punch me." He backed away from me, a

smile on his face.

"You don't mean really punch you, do you?" I furrowed my brow.

"Nothing bad will happen if you do."

Except, I'd feel bad, even if I didn't hurt him.

But this was just supposed to be a game, right?

Nothing serious.

I advanced toward him, but he was quick enough to get out of my way. When I swung toward him, he evaded with ease.

"I think you've had too much practice." I tried again.

Oliver didn't move, but he blocked my punch.

And then he caught me in his arms, pulling me to him.

"Hey!" I let out a laugh as he tickled me.

I managed to turn around in his embrace and face him, but he caught my wrists in a tight grip.

"What are you going to do now?" He grinned.

I stared deep into his eyes, and then I kissed him.

His grip on me loosened as his lips moved against mine, and I tapped my fist against his shoulder.

He let out a laugh as he pulled away from me. "That was terrible."

"Well, I don't want to hurt you."

"You can kiss me again instead." He wound his arms around me, and I wrapped mine around his neck.

"Yeah, I'd like that better." I pressed my lips against his.

A phone buzzed somewhere, and I tensed.

"Ignore it," he whispered before kissing me again.

Heat spread through me as his hands lowered to my ass and squeezed.

He tugged on my shirt, and I lifted my arms so he could take it off me. His fingers caught the clasp of my bra as he kissed me again.

He spun me around and I braced myself against the wall. His lips brushed my shoulder, and then he left a trail of hot kisses down my back as he kneaded my breasts and pinched my nipples.

I groaned as his hands glided down my body. His fingers hooked into the waistband of my pants and underwear, and in one swift move, he pulled them down.

When he nudged my legs apart, he pressed his lips to my inner thigh.

My whole body was on fire, and my breath left me in little gasps as his mouth moved to my center.

His tongue traced my opening, lapping at me, and then he dipped it inside me. He licked and gently sucked at my clit, and my knees almost gave out.

Every flick of his tongue brought me closer to my release, and when my orgasm hit me, I let out a groan.

When Oliver let go of me, I leaned on the wall, gasping for breath. I heard him move behind me, and a few moments later, I felt his cock pushing at my entrance.

He rubbed himself along my opening, making me hiss, and then he plunged inside me. I cried out as he thrust into me, gripping my hips.

Maybe I should be worried someone would see or hear us, but I decided that I didn't care.

The phone was buzzing again, but it sounded so distant that I barely even heard it.

Oliver pounded into me, diving as deep as possible inside me.

Every inch of me tingled with delight, and my moans grew louder.

When he slammed himself inside me with a powerful thrust, I shattered into a million pieces of endless pleasure.

I let out a cry, and he groaned, pressing himself against me, his cock buried deep inside me.

If this whole thing between us was a mistake, I didn't want to know it.

I just wanted to enjoy this, whatever it was.

But when I turned to face Oliver and met his eyes, I had a feeling that maybe this could be so much more than just sex.

CHAPTER TWENTY-TWO

"WE LOST ONE OF OUR stash houses," Romano said.

"How the fuck did that happen?" I asked.

"The guards spotted a strange guy lurking close by. The guy was probably a spy. They tried to call you to ask for your permission to go after him, but you weren't picking up your phone. By the time they decided to call me, it was too late. Vitrianni's men were already there."

I closed my eyes for a moment. "Fuck."

Nerea and I had been busy. I hadn't thought it was anything important.

I'd been wrong.

"Everyone's also waiting for your approval for our latest project," he said.

I frowned at him.

"The houses you wanted me to buy and then use for—"

"Yes, yes." Now I remembered.

I'd been spending a lot of time with Nerea lately, and I'd forgotten to do a few things.

That wasn't good at all.

I didn't do distractions.

I didn't do things that could slow down my climb to the top.

And Nerea...

"If you're occupied with something else, I can take care of it," Romano said. "I understand if your priorities changed—"

"No." I met his gaze. "I'll deal with it. Actually, get my apartment ready. It'll be easier to catch up on everything from there."

I needed to get away from Nerea.

She was too tempting.

I couldn't let anyone get in the way of my goal.

Not even her.

Especially not her.

I had to get my mind back on what truly mattered. Spending time with Nerea and having some fun was nice, but I wasn't about to ruin everything because of...

I didn't even know what it was.

My business came before everything.

I had no idea how I'd managed to forget that.

"You'll be in charge of keeping my wife safe while I'm gone," I said.

Romano nodded.

"She can do whatever she wants, as long as she doesn't leave this house."

"Understood."

Putting some much-needed distance between Nerea and me would be good for both of us.

It was time to go back to the real world.

CHAPTER TWENTY-THREE

Nerea

"CAN YOU TELL ME WHERE Oliver is?" I asked one of his men because I hadn't seen Oliver for over a day.

"No. Sorry, ma'am."

"Do you know when he'll be back?"

He shook his head.

I let out a sigh and headed back to my room. Now I had everything. I could watch TV, play games, and even go online.

But something was missing.

Oliver.

Everything was more fun when he was with me, and I supposed I'd gotten used to having him with me.

Now that he was gone, it seemed weird.

But why hadn't he told me anything? Why had he just vanished?

It was one of the things I'd hoped he'd never do to me.

Had I said something?

Done something?

Maybe he'd just grown tired of me.

Maybe he'd found something better to do, or someone better to spend his time with.

And I was all alone once again.

Maybe one day, I'd stop losing people, and they'd stop abandoning me.

But I supposed today wasn't one of those days.

Getting used to people and getting attached to them was a terrible, terrible thing. It always left me with this big hole in my chest.

I spotted a phone and picked it up. Surprisingly

enough, it unlocked for me. I searched through the contacts for Oliver's number.

If he was done with me, he could at least tell me that and not leave me here waiting for something that was never going to happen.

I dialed his number.

It kept ringing and ringing.

But Oliver didn't pick up.

He was too busy for me.

Too busy to even tell me that himself.

Tears prickled the corners of my eyes, and I hated the way I was feeling, but I couldn't help it.

I'd started to care about Oliver, despite everything.

I should've known better than to fall for a mafia boss.

Oliver

I STARED AT THE SCREEN of my phone and all the missed calls from Nerea.

What the fuck was I doing?

She had to have a billion questions, and I'd just left her.

I'd run like a coward.

It wasn't like me.

Nerea deserved better.

But what should I tell her? How could I even explain that she was too much of a distraction for me?

Even though we weren't in the same building, I still had trouble focusing, and I couldn't stop thinking about her.

It wouldn't surprise me if she hated me. She'd probably hated me all along and was biding her time until our contract was over.

The time we'd spent together didn't mean anything to her.

She was probably bored without me.

But I wanted to see her.

I wanted to kiss her.

And I didn't want to stay at my apartment for a moment longer.

I had to see her.

Now.

Even if it was a mistake.

THE DOOR TO NEREA'S room was cracked open, and I pushed it wide.

Nerea looked up at me from the floor where she was sitting. She'd brought a TV to her room and was watching one of her shows.

"You're back," she said, her face serious, her voice devoid of all emotion.

"I am." I inched closer to her, unsure what to say.

Should I apologize?

Try to explain?

Should I pretend nothing happened?

I always knew what to do, but now I was clueless. Giving orders and taking care of my business was easy compared to this. The only thing I knew was that I didn't want Nerea to look at me the way she was looking at me now.

She pushed herself up to her feet and turned off the TV. "What do you want?"

"We could watch one of your shows." Maybe after that, I'd know what to say to her to make things right.

"Why?" She crossed her arms.

"Why not?"

She huffed. "Do you really think you can just come back here and act like nothing happened?"

"You're mad at me."

"Of course I'm mad at you!" She raised her voice.

"You just left without saying anything. You didn't answer any of my calls! And now you're back, as if nothing happened. You don't get to do that, Oliver."

"I had work to do. I was busy." I moved closer to her.

"So busy that you couldn't talk to me for a few minutes? I don't believe it."

"I'm not used to any of this." It was the truth.

She snorted. "Oh, that's just a lovely excuse."

I was almost willing to say anything she wanted me to say just to see her smile again.

Just to stop her from being mad at me.

What was she doing to me?

My gaze lowered to her lips. Right now, all I could think about was kissing her.

"Maybe I can make it up to you," I said, and then I couldn't stop myself anymore.

My mouth collided with hers.

She melted into my kiss, and I realized just how much I'd missed her.

I'd missed her company.

I'd missed her soft lips.

I'd missed her.

Nerea

I SHOULD PUSH OLIVER away and tell him he couldn't play with me like this.

But I'd missed him so damn much, and he was back now. Maybe he really hadn't understood what he'd done.

I didn't think he'd ever been in an actual relationship

or knew how to do something that wasn't related to his business.

But that still didn't make it right.

I should make him understand that.

Except, I couldn't stop kissing him.

Maybe later, once I quenched the thirst raging inside me.

His kiss was full of hunger, his hands ripping at my clothes.

It looked like he'd missed me too, and I was glad about it.

I caught his shirt, yanking it open and letting the buttons pop out. He pulled my shirt over my head and tossed it aside, his hand trailing up my bare stomach.

I shoved him toward the bed, and he let himself fall on it. After I got my pants and underwear off as fast as possible, I climbed on top of him and undid his belt.

Oliver watched me with desire burning in his eyes, his lips parted.

He tried to catch my hands, but I didn't let him.

I unbuttoned his pants and tugged his underwear down, freeing his erection. My patience had completely run out, so I positioned myself over him and guided him inside me.

We both groaned as I slid myself down on him, taking him all in.

I placed my hand against his chest, keeping him down as I rocked my hips.

As I impaled myself on him over and over again, I threw my head back and let out a loud moan.

At that moment, I hated him.

I hated him for making me feel so good.

I hated him because he had this strange effect on me.

But at the same time, I didn't really hate him.

It was completely messed up.

I slammed myself down on him and groaned as my orgasm overcame my whole body, leaving me breathless.

Oliver grunted, and I leaned toward him so I could press my lips against his.

I pulled away from him and threw myself on the bed next to him, trying to catch my breath.

"Are you going to leave now?" I asked as he shifted.

"Nerea—" He lay on his side as his gaze met mine.

"No, don't. If this is just about sex for you, then tell me that."

"I—"

"Oliver!" someone shouted in the hallway, and I grabbed the sheets, wrapping them around me.

Oliver quickly sat up and found his underwear.

"What is it, Romano?" he asked.

"You need to come with me. Quickly! There's an

urgent matter we need to take care of. I'm afraid it can't wait."

"All right. I'm coming!" Oliver glanced at me. "I'm really sorry about this."

"Go. We'll talk later." I supposed I couldn't ask a mafia boss to put his business on hold for me.

I didn't know how dire the situation was, but people could get killed.

Bad things could happen.

As Oliver got dressed and rushed for the door, I let out a sigh.

No one in their right mind would want to date a mafia boss, and I had no idea what I was even doing here or what I expected would happen.

CHAPTER TWENTY-SIX

"WHAT'S GOING ON?" I asked.

Romano had a grave expression on his face. "It's Clive. I have information that he's going to publish an article with proof that you're a mafia boss."

"What? How? Are you sure this isn't another one of

Vitrianni's games? Do you trust your source?" I didn't want us to fall into my enemy's trap.

"I trust my source," Romano said. "I can tell you all about him if you want—"

"We don't have time for that. I trust you. Do you know what kind of proof Clive has?"

"He interviewed someone who works or worked for you."

"We have a traitor in our midst?"

"It seems so, yes."

"I want our most trusted men to figure out who it is."

"Yes, of course," Romano said.

"But it's just an interview. Is it anonymous? How does Clive plan to prove that this interview isn't completely made up?"

"I don't know that. My source couldn't figure it out. There's also something else."

"What?"

"It's about your wife." Romano licked his lips. "There's a photo of her and you. At the hotel."

I creased my brow. "A photo? What kind of photo?"

"It's from that time when you went to a business dinner together."

"Why would a photo from the business dinner be a problem?"

"Because it's not from the dinner itself. It's from

security camera footage. Apparently, you have Nerea against the wall, and it could be interpreted as if you're trying to hurt her."

I groaned. "That's insane. We were making out."

"My source tells me it doesn't look that way. I know you could say it's all a lie, but we don't know what kind of information the traitor spilled. It might be something that could be dangerous for us or seriously affect our business. If the information is real and the cops show up on our doorstep, Clive will be the least of our problems."

If only one of the things in that damn article turned out to be true, people would have doubts and start believing the rest of the things, even if they were lies.

I'd lose the Catrona deal for sure, and who knew how many other deals.

The cops could start sniffing around more too, or they might even come for me.

"The article hasn't been published yet, right?" I said.

Romano nodded.

"Then we can stop this and find out what's really going on."

He pulled out his phone and took a look at the screen. "Yes, there's still time."

"We can destroy everything they might have already printed out and make sure they don't print any more."

"There's an online edition of the article too."

"Find someone who can hack into the newspaper's website, take it down, and keep it that way for as long as we need it."

"What should we do about Clive? He has to have a copy of the article. If he publishes it on his own and sells it to someone else—"

"Wait. If Clive really had something big on me, then why even bother publishing it? Why not just hand over all the evidence to the cops?"

"We still haven't figured out whose side he's on. He might be looking for an article that's going to launch his career into the stratosphere. If he just gives all the evidence to the cops, he gets nothing. Maybe only a small mention somewhere, but nothing as big as if he publishes an exclusive."

I shook my head. "Something's off about the whole thing. Clive would be more careful if he was only looking for his special career-changing article. He wouldn't let anyone except his boss see it. He would just get it printed and publish it online when the time came, if he was crazy enough to risk pissing me off like that. I don't know if his boss would even agree to publish something like that either without taking some serious precautions."

"What are you thinking?"

"This is just a distraction. It has to be. Vitrianni is

behind all this. He's planning something. Maybe another attack. If I go down because of some stupid article, it will be bad for his business too because there'll be too many cops prowling the city. He'd have to lie low and would lose a lot of money, which would only weaken him. His best option is to defeat me without the cops or anyone else getting involved, but he knows he's not strong enough to do that in an open war, so he needs to play dirty to get what he wants."

It had to be a trap. It was the only thing that made sense in this mess. Random reporters, no matter how popular they thought they were, didn't just go after a mafia boss like that.

They might publish all they had after the mafia boss in question was arrested, but not before. None of them were stupid enough to put a target on their backs, especially when there was no benefit worth dying for.

"We don't know for sure if Clive and Vitrianni—" Romano said.

"We don't, but we don't have any time left to figure it out. I think Vitrianni knows I'll try to stop the article and go after the newspaper. I don't know if he expects to catch me there by surprise and try to kill me, or if he's planning to hit me somewhere else to try to weaken me while he knows my men and I are busy."

"You believe Clive leaked the news about the article because he knew someone would tell you?"

"I do."

"What are we going to do? If we do nothing, that article might get published."

"We're not going to do *nothing*. I have a plan." I didn't know if it would work, but even if I was wrong, I could still get two birds with one stone.

"Prepare two teams," I said. "One smaller, and one bigger. We're going to go after the newspaper and see if there's anything to stop, but we're going to be very careful about it, in case it's a trap. I'll pretend I'm going with the smaller team, but I'll slip away and join the bigger team. Then we're going to attack Vitrianni where he least expects it. His men are probably going to be on their way to attack me, so they'll have to rush back. We can use that. Kill as many of them as we can."

"What if you're wrong about Vitrianni's plan? We don't have a way to confirm your theory."

"If I'm wrong, the smaller team can stop the article, and our attack on Vitrianni might be less successful, but it's high time for payback anyway."

"I'll get the teams ready," Romano said.

"There's something else I want. The attack on the newspaper has to be super clean, and by that, I mean we can't leave any traces that will lead to us. We hide our symbols. We hide everything that might help the cops or anyone else to identify us."

"Of course."

"Have someone track down Clive. I'm done with this shit. He's going down, and I don't care even if he's friends with the most powerful people in the whole world. No one's untouchable."

I'd let all of this go on for too long.

But now, it was time to end it.

And maybe after that, I'd figure out what to do about Nerea.

CHAPTER TWENTY-SEVEN

Nerea

"WHAT'S GOING ON?" I rushed after Oliver as he was on his way to the door. For the past hour, Oliver had been running around and kept talking to someone on his phone. His men seemed to be on the move too, and there was something different in the air—like some invisible tension that had enveloped everyone.

"I don't have time to explain," he said.

"Is it about—"

He turned to me, annoyance filling his eyes. "I said, I don't have time right now. You'll be safe here, so you have nothing to worry about. We'll talk when I get back."

He strode away from me, and I inwardly groaned.

While I could understand that he was busy and in a hurry because he had some important business to handle, I doubted he couldn't spare a second or two to tell me what was going on.

Maybe he just wasn't used to having to explain himself to anyone, and yeah, I knew that every second counted if there was danger, but I didn't think it would've hurt if he'd just told me where he was going.

I didn't even know if I was supposed to be worried about him. Was his life going to be in danger?

He sounded so confident about returning and talking to me, but what if he didn't come back? I didn't want to think about the worst-case scenario, but if there was something between us—and even if there wasn't— shouldn't I at least be in on the things that went on?

Oliver dying out there would affect me in a big way. Didn't he think I'd be worried sick about him the whole time he was gone? Did he even consider that I might care about what happened to him?

I bet his men knew what to do in case something happened. They had plans and everything, and Oliver just expected me to sit here and wait as if nothing at all was going on.

I didn't like any of that.

Maybe he even had some kind of plan for me, but he hadn't told me anything about it.

Would he ever be able to see me as his partner, or would he always think that I'd do exactly what he wanted me to do without question?

Would he ever consider my feelings and see that I was more than capable of handling whatever the hell was going on?

After all, if something went wrong, I wanted to be the one to decide what I wanted to do next.

I looked through the window, just as Oliver was going for his car. My stomach immediately tightened with anxiety.

Something could really happen to him out there, and I wouldn't even know about it until someone decided to tell me.

That just felt wrong on so many levels. Sure, I couldn't go out there with him, but that didn't mean he could just leave me like this. I wasn't one of his men who was here just to follow orders and who would find another employer if things went to hell.

I chewed on the inside of my cheek.

Could our relationship ever work out if things remained the way they were now?

I didn't think so.

But was Oliver willing to do something to change that?

That was up to him to decide. Maybe then I'd finally found out if I meant something to him or not.

I WAS WITH TEAM A THAT was going to pay a visit to the newspaper headquarters, and I was about to slip away from them so that I could join the attack on Vitrianni when my phone buzzed.

Romano's number was on the screen.

"What's going on?" I asked.

"We know where Clive is, but there's a problem."

"Why? Where is he?" I didn't like the sound of that.

"He's at the airport. It might not be easy to get to him without causing a scene."

"Don't worry about that. I'll handle it." I swerved and stepped on the gas pedal so I could get to the airport as soon as possible.

Clive had to be thinking that I'd be busy and that he'd manage to slip away before anyone could catch him, but I wasn't about to let that happen.

My men might be too obvious if they rushed the airport, but I could sneak around on my own without a problem.

Yeah, I'd be without any protection, with only myself to count on, and there was a chance this was a trap too.

But I doubted Vitrianni and Clive would expect I'd go after Clive on my own, and it wasn't easy to stage an attack at the airport with so many witnesses and cameras around. If there was a shootout, the cops would be all over it.

It didn't take me long to reach the airport. After I parked my car in the busy parking lot, I got out and grabbed a baseball cap I had in the back.

Slipping the cap on my head, I hurried inside.

The airport was brimming with people.

I scanned the crowd.

Where was Clive?

I stalked through the crowd, and then I spotted him.

He was sitting in one of the chairs, surrounded by people.

How could I get to him without anyone noticing?

I lowered my cap and inched closer while I kept an eye on him. For what seemed like forever, he didn't move from his seat.

Fuck.

He knew he was perfectly safe here because everyone would see if someone approached him, and he'd see me too if I tried going closer.

Maybe he didn't think I'd go after him because he and Vitrianni both expected I'd have better things to do, or that I would be losing my mind over the article.

Since Clive had made everyone believe the article was already ready to be published, he probably thought going after him wasn't my priority.

Just when I started wondering if he was ever going to get up, he rose to his feet. I followed him, keeping my head down.

When he glanced over his shoulder, I ducked behind a group of people.

He kept going, and it looked like he was walking in the direction of the restroom.

A smile spread across my lips.

That was just perfect.

Once Clive entered the restroom, I looked around before pulling out my gun with a silencer.

A man walked out of the restroom, and I used the opportunity to slip inside and jam the door with a piece of metal.

Clive was alone.

What an idiot.

But he was probably just a reporter who'd gotten involved in something he shouldn't have, and Vitrianni had used him and conveniently failed to tell him about the danger he'd really be in. If Clive had never had a gun pressed to his head, he could've underestimated the gravity of the situation.

I pointed my gun at him.

He saw my reflection in the mirror, his eyes widening, but it was too late.

I pulled the trigger.

The bullet got him in the back of the head, and he collapsed to the floor.

I tucked my gun back under my jacket and crouched next to him.

I pulled Clive's dress shirt open, looking for something.

Proof that I'd been right all along.

And then I spotted it.

Vitrianni's tattoo—a very small one—was on his side. It wouldn't surprise me if Vitrianni had made him believe that he was one of his men and that he'd always be protected.

Vitrianni was going to get what he deserved for starting this shit up.

I let go of Clive and rose to my feet, and then I carefully freed the door and strode out of there before anyone could see me. Since Clive had that tattoo, I doubted anyone would be looking too hard for his killer.

The cops would conclude this was all just a part of some mafia war and leave it at that.

Clive's CIA friend—if there was one—would probably pretend Clive had never existed.

A dead man was of no use to anyone.

Once I was back in my car, I dialed Romano's number.

"Any news?" I asked, but since he'd answered, I knew that he wasn't busy, unless I was about to hear someone else's voice from the other end of the line.

"Yes, the situation with the newspaper has been handled. You were right. There was no proof and no article. Well, there was an article about you, but only more nonsense. We got out of there before anyone got hurt. I don't have an update for the Vitrianni situation just yet, but I should soon."

"Good. Our annoying reporter is no longer a problem."

"I see."

"I'm on my way to join the guys." We hadn't had too much time to prepare our attack, so my men didn't have an easy task, but I was confident we wouldn't fail.

"I don't think that's a good idea. You're the boss, and this attack isn't something you should risk—"

I was about to say that yes, I was the boss, and it wasn't like me to hide somewhere and stay away while my men fought for me, but then I remembered something else.

Nerea.

I hadn't even thought about setting up a plan for her in case something happened to me. It was something I hadn't considered before.

The question was, why did I care?

She'd figure something out, or whoever became boss after me would kill her.

I gritted my teeth at that thought. If someone wanted what was mine, there'd be no way I'd let them hurt Nerea.

"You're right," I finally said. "But if they need backup, let me know."

There was a quick intake of breath on the other end of the line. "Of course."

I was glad Romano had decided not to comment on my decision.

It was strange to sit back and wait, but if anything happened to Nerea because I got myself killed, it would be all my fault, and I couldn't have that.

Once this was over, I'd have to tell Romano to come up with a plan that would ensure Nerea's safety.

PACED UP AND DOWN the room. I knew Oliver was probably in the middle of a fight and that he knew what he was doing, but I couldn't find a way to calm myself down.

Was this how all mafia wives felt?

Were they constantly worrying if their husbands

were going to come back home alive from their missions or was it just me?

I kept checking the news for any information, even though I hoped there wouldn't be any. If Oliver got caught, I supposed the cops would come for me too.

I ran my hand over my face.

Oh hell.

I so didn't like any of this.

I didn't want a life like this.

It was too nerve-racking. Even if Oliver had shared more details with me, I didn't think I'd feel any better right now. Hell, maybe I'd be even more worried.

But then I heard a familiar name and looked up at the screen.

A reporter was saying that Clive Willis had been found dead in the airport's restroom. A witness had mentioned he'd seen a suspicious man with a baseball cap, but so far, the cops didn't have any information about the killer.

The reporter spoke about Clive's possible involvement with the mafia and then mentioned that the cops were investigating the newspaper Clive had worked for.

I chewed on the inside of my cheek.

Was Oliver going to get caught in the middle of all this? Why did he even have to do any of it? Had he really had to kill Clive? Had he done it himself or had he let one of his men do it?

But then I heard the noise of car engines, and I rushed to the closest window, my heart racing.

It wasn't the cops.

Oliver got out of one of the cars, a smile on his face.

Relief hit me like a truck, and then I scowled.

He was fine, and he was laughing with his men, probably about his successful mission.

Once he entered, he spotted me immediately.

"Hey," he said softly.

I wanted to throw myself into his arms and kiss him, but I held back.

We still hadn't had a chance to talk, and I didn't even know what we were to each other.

What was our status?

Were we just two people bound by a contract who liked spending time together from time to time?

Or were we something more?

"What happened? I heard it on the news that Clive's dead."

"*That* happened," Oliver said. "He was one of my enemy's men, or at least he'd been helping my enemy for some reason. I stopped their attempt to undermine me in the race for a very important contract. I hit my enemy too. I wish I could've been with my men, but let's just say many of my enemy's men are dead."

"Is that supposed to be good news?" I asked.

"Yes." He furrowed his brow.

"Are you done with it all now then? Will you be able to focus on your legit business more now that your enemy is weakened? Or maybe, after you get that contract?"

His frown deepened. "My enemy is still out there. Nothing's done yet. And no, I'll keep things the way they are. Why would I change anything?"

"You could have enough money and power even if you weren't a mafia boss, and you could have something else too: a chance at a normal life."

He laughed. "I wasn't born to lead a normal life."

"So that's it? That's your decision?"

"Yes. Why are you so serious? We should celebrate." A smile broke out on his face.

"I have nothing to celebrate. While I waited for you, I realized that I don't like this. I don't like any of this. I wasn't born to be a wife of a mafia boss. I can't just sit here and wait while you're out there doing who knows what, and I don't even know if you're going to return!"

His smile faded. "I get that, and I'm working on a plan for you in case something happens to me."

I stared at him. "Are you serious right now? A plan if

something happens to you? Is that supposed to make me feel better?"

"I thought it would." Confusion filled his eyes.

"You don't get it, Oliver, do you?"

"Get what?"

"When you're gone, I don't worry about myself. I worry about you!"

His lips parted in surprise.

"I don't think you understand the concept that if you died, people would miss you. People would cry for you. People would feel—No, I would feel. I would feel like my heart was parted in two. Would you be able to sit and wait while someone you care about is doing something dangerous? And you don't know anything about it and can't even be with them?"

"If you want to know what I'm doing, I can—"

I shook my head. "It's not just about that."

"I can't change who I am and what I do. If you can't accept that, then I don't know what to tell you."

"Are you sure about that? What's stopping you from turning your business completely legit? You can have whatever you want anyway. It's not like you'll have things to do with all that money. Hell, you might not even live long enough to spend any of it because of what you do."

"I told you already that I can't do that. My life isn't

always at risk. The situation today is different. Once I defeat Vitrianni once and for all, the city will be mine, and there will be peace."

"Peace? Yeah, maybe for you, because you're the boss. What about all the other people?"

He cocked his head at me. "What's your problem with people like me? What I do doesn't affect you or any people like you."

I let out a strangled laugh. "My parents died because of the mafia!"

"What? How?" Surprise laced his voice. "I thought they died in a house fire."

"They did, but guess what? Do you know why the fire started? An electrical fault, they said. But my grandparents knew. The company that built my parents' house belonged to the mafia. Apparently, they stole some of the material that my dad had bought, and they thought no one would notice or care."

"I'm sorry to hear that, but mistakes happen and bad people exist. My companies don't do botched jobs."

"That's not the point. I guess I just don't know how to explain it to you that you'd be better off if you dropped the mafia part of your business."

"You're mad at me right now. We can talk some other time." He reached out for me, but I stepped away from him.

"There's nothing to talk about." I'd made my decision.

Maybe it wasn't late for me to protect myself and my heart.

Even if the thought of breaking things off with Oliver hurt like hell.

But he was never going to understand or change, and maybe I just didn't know how to help him to get there.

Maybe it was better for both of us to end this now.

"All right." It was all he said before he walked away.

"IS EVERYTHING OKAY?" Romano asked.

No, it fucking wasn't.

I might have won tonight, but I'd lost too.

I'd lost Nerea, and for some reason, that completely eclipsed my win.

I didn't think talking to her was going to change

anything. She and I weren't compatible because she wanted and needed something that I could never give her: a regular life.

"Are you already thinking about the war with Vitrianni?" Romano asked. "We all know there's no going back now. We need to defeat him once and for all."

"Yeah, we do."

But first I had to do something.

Wars were dangerous, and they could take a long time until they ended.

Vitrianni wouldn't go down easily.

I was sure of it.

And Nerea didn't deserve to be caught in all this shit, especially if the cops got involved.

"Vitrianni suffered a huge blow, but I don't think we can deal with him in time to take him out of the race for the Catrona deal. We have to hope the board members will make the right decision, or we can try to find some other way to sway them," Romano said.

"I'm sure Vitrianni would've already found some blackmail material if there was any. We need to be careful with this deal." I went to pour myself a glass of whiskey.

"There's something I need you to do for me," I added. "Nerea shouldn't be here when everything goes down. With Clive gone, we can control the rest of the reporters. I don't need her with me anymore. I want you to arrange a trip to Spain for her."

"Do you want her to have an accident or—"

I spun toward Romano, baring my teeth. "Absolutely not. What the fuck is wrong with you?"

"I apologize," he said, surprise flickering through his eyes. "I thought you wanted to make sure she wouldn't talk. Do you have another use for her?"

"No, I don't."

Romano's eyes widened even more. "Then why do you—"

"It's what I want." I took a gulp of the whiskey.

I'd never done anything like this before. If Nerea left, I'd get nothing out of it. She'd be a risk.

But she'd be safe.

She'd get a chance at a happy life she wanted and deserved.

A life without me in it.

The smartest thing to do here would be to kill her. She knew too much about me and about what I'd done. If she talked to the wrong people, it could destroy everything.

My whole life's work.

Unless she was too afraid of me to do something like that.

But I was still taking an unnecessary risk, and I didn't know why.

Or maybe I did.

Was that uncomfortable feeling in my chest what people talked about when they spoke about love?

I didn't believe in that shit.

I didn't believe in doing things for free and without any benefit for me.

I'd never released anyone from their contract before it was up.

And yet, I had to let Nerea go.

I couldn't imagine this world without her.

I couldn't bring myself to kill her or be the cause of her death.

Maybe I'd been wrong.

Maybe love did exist.

But why did it have to hurt so fucking much?

CHAPTER THIRTY-ONE

Nerea

OLIVER DIDN'T EVEN come to say goodbye, but maybe it was better like that because I didn't know if I could leave otherwise.

Romano had taken me to the airport, and once I boarded the plane, I could barely stop myself from bursting into tears.

Oliver and I weren't meant to be.

We wanted different things in life.

We belonged to two different worlds.

He could be a good person. I knew that. But I didn't think he'd let himself be one.

I hoped that one day, I could move on and forget about him.

He'd rescinded our contract and given me the money anyway, or at least that was what Romano had said.

When the plane landed, I took a deep breath, hoping that I was ready for a new adventure. At least I could fulfill my grandma's wish and meet my relatives, but first I had to find a place to stay and then try to find them.

Too bad I didn't have the box she'd wanted me to give them with me, but I supposed I could get it some other time.

Oliver had wanted me out of his city and his life as soon as possible, so I hadn't had a chance to go back to my apartment first.

Once I got my bag, I made my way toward the exit, but there was a group of people holding up a sheet of paper with my name on it.

When a dark-haired woman saw me, she pointed at me and said something in a language I couldn't understand. The others looked at me too.

A teenage girl got to me first.

"Hi, you must be Nerea," she said. "I'm Amaia. We've been waiting for you."

"For me?"

She nodded. "My great-grandmother was your grandmother's older sister, or something like that. I'm terrible with family trees. Anyway, as soon as we were told you were coming, we couldn't wait to meet you. Let me introduce you to my parents and my aunt and her family."

"Someone told you I was coming?" I could barely believe it.

I'd thought I'd be staying at a hotel and then have to find my relatives on my own.

"Yeah. Some guy called. My grandma didn't understand a word he said because she doesn't speak English, so she hung up the phone. Luckily, I answered the second time he called. He explained who you were and all, and we said we'd be happy to meet you and help you with anything you might need."

"Ma'am, you forgot this!" someone yelled.

I turned around.

A man was holding the box with the things my grandma had prepared for my relatives. How the hell had that gotten here?

Had I told Oliver about it? I must have.

And he'd remembered.

Tears filled the corners of my eyes.

Maybe he did care about me, after all.

"Thanks," I said to the man and eyed him for a moment.

Had Oliver sent someone to protect me too? How could this man know who I was?

My name was on the box, though, and the woman who I assumed was Amaia's mother was still holding that sheet of paper with my name, so I couldn't be sure.

"Let me introduce you to everyone," Amaia said.

"I'd love that." A smile spread across my lips.

CHAPTER THIRTY-TWO

"VITRIANNI THINKS HE can avoid the war," Romano said. "I have information that he's going to offer you a deal."

I snorted. "As if I'd ever sign a deal with him after what he tried to pull, especially because even he knows he's going to lose."

"I think I know how we can get him." Romano kept talking, but my phone buzzed.

I glanced at the screen.

It was a text from the guy I'd sent to keep an eye on Nerea. He wanted me to know that she was perfectly fine.

A small smile stretched across my lips.

That was good.

Nerea was strong. She'd do fine on her own. If only I could see her right now.

But I couldn't spy on her. It wouldn't be fair.

I missed her so fucking much.

"What do you think?" Romano asked.

"What?" I looked up at him, pocketing my phone.

"Have you heard any of what I said?"

"No."

He shook his head at me. "Do you have a plan of attack?"

"I do." Dragging this whole thing out would make no sense.

I was losing money and time on Vitrianni for no good reason.

"Can we narrow down Vitrianni's location?" I asked.

"Yes, but he's holed up in one of his hideouts, and it won't be easy to find him. We'll probably have to attack a lot of his safe houses and stash houses before we get to him."

"That's good enough. I bet he's scared. If we form four groups and attack Vitrianni's men from all sides, he'll run. All we have to do is figure out which route out of the city he's most likely to take."

"I'll get a map," Romano said. "I'm sure we can try to guess where he'll go, but he might get alerted of our presence if we try to ambush him. His scout will probably go first and might see us."

"That's why we'll attack him from more than one place. We'll take out his guards first, and just when he thinks he's escaped, I'll be waiting for him."

I was looking forward to it all.

MY PHONE BUZZED, AND I smiled when I read the text I'd gotten. Vitrianni was racing straight toward me.

I'd turned off my car lights and waited in the darkness. The road was empty, like it was almost every night after midnight, and, everywhere around it, there were just fields and trees, which was good. There was less chance something would go wrong or that someone would get in the way.

Once I spotted lights in the distance speeding toward me, I braced myself, and when they got closer, I started my car and stopped it right in the middle of the road.

Vitrianni swerved, the tires screeching, and skidded off the road. I got out of my car, my gun ready in my hand.

Vitrianni's car came to a stop after a loud crash against a tree. Vitrianni stumbled out of the car as I pointed my gun at him.

"Hi, Vitrianni," I said.

He spun around, his eyes going wide.

I flashed him a smile as I pulled the trigger.

"You shouldn't have gotten in my way," I said to his dead body, and headed back to my car.

EVERYWHERE AROUND ME, my men were celebrating or shouting to congratulate me.

I kept a smile on my face, but I didn't feel it at all.

"Congratulations," Romano said when he saw me, clapping me on the back. "I knew you'd make it one day, but I didn't think it would be this soon. You own the city now, and your biggest contestant for the Catrona deal is dead."

"Yeah." I made my way to the table with drinks and poured myself a glass of whiskey.

This was supposed to be the happiest day of my life.

I finally had everything I'd ever wanted.

But my win tasted as shitty as this fucking whiskey.

"Are you going to give the men who fought a few days off so they could celebrate with their families too?" Romano asked.

"Yes, sure. Why not?" I headed to the terrace.

Everyone had someone. Someone they could share their happiness with. And I was back here, all alone.

And Nerea was miles, and miles, and miles away from me.

"Do you need anything before I leave?" Romano asked behind my back.

I turned toward him.

I did need something.

Someone.

My wife.

She'd told me once that none of this would matter if I was alone in the end. There was something money and power couldn't buy: that damn smile on her face when she looked at me.

Now, I only wanted her.

But was it too late? Would she be willing to give me a second chance?

"I need you to do something for me," I said. "I'm going to Spain."

The corners of Romano's lips tilted up. "I'll arrange everything."

"Thank you." I downed the rest of my whiskey.

Nerea

WITH OLIVER'S MONEY, I'd bought myself a nice little house on the same street where my relatives lived.

It was really nice here, and I loved the peace and quiet I had. My house was perfect too, and I had everything that I needed.

My relatives were all wonderful people too.

And yet, nothing could fill the void in my heart.

I often wondered what Oliver was doing and if he was fine. Like an idiot, I kept checking the news.

It seemed like he was more than okay because, this morning, there was an article mentioning that he'd gotten a super important deal that would bring him huge benefits because his main competitor had wound up dead.

Apparently, the competitor had been a mafia boss, so the board members were happy to have avoided closing a deal with the mafia. If only they knew they'd only awarded their precious contract to another mafia boss. Maybe I shouldn't find that funny, but I did.

A little.

The doorbell rang.

It had to be Amaia. She loved to stop by after school and tell me fun stories about her family.

I opened the door with a smile on my face.

My heart skipped a beat, my smile fading as my eyes widened.

Maybe I was dreaming or hallucinating.

Oliver stood in front of me, as handsome as ever, a small smile on his face.

"Hey," he said softly.

"Um, hey. What are you doing here?" I eyed him carefully.

"I came to see you. Can I come in?"

"Sure." I moved away from the door, unsure what to think.

The last thing I wanted was to get my hopes up for nothing. Maybe he just happened to be in the area and wanted to see what I'd spent his money on.

Or, hell, what if he wanted some of it back?

"Nice house," he said, looking around.

"It is."

"Are you seeing someone?" His gaze locked on mine.

"No. Why?" I hadn't expected that to be one of his first questions.

"Because I came here to say something to you. Something important."

I gave him an expectant look.

"I love you, Nerea," he said. "I know this sounds weird coming from me, but I realized that my life is nothing without you in it. I have everything I've ever wanted, but it seems meaningless now because I don't have you."

My mouth fell open as I could barely believe what I'd just heard.

"I came here hoping... Hoping that there's a chance you still feel something for me. I didn't understand what you were trying to tell me before, until I defeated my enemy. Everyone was happy. Everyone. But I didn't feel anything. I just missed you."

I bit down on my lip.

I'd had no idea how much I'd longed for him to say those words until now.

But there was something else...

"What does that mean?" I asked softly. "I do have feelings for you, but I still don't want to be the wife of a mafia boss."

"You don't have to be. I just want to be with you, and if that means I have to leave everything in Romano's hands and stay here with you, I'll accept that offer immediately, without even thinking."

"Are you sure?" I gaped at him.

"I am."

I took a shuddery breath, wondering what to do. Even if he stayed here with me and left his position in the mafia to someone else or ran his business remotely, I didn't know if I could do this.

Bad things could still happen.

He could be taken away from me.

Or he could change his mind about me.

But I couldn't keep being afraid of ending up alone forever, or I was really going to end up alone. It would be like a self-fulfilling prophecy.

Did I dare to take this step?

Was I finally brave enough?

Yes, I was.

"All right," I said, feeling lighter than I'd felt in years.

A smile broke out on Oliver's face, and then he closed the distance between us and kissed me with so much passion that I couldn't think about anything other than him.

Nerea

OLIVER WRAPPED HIS arms around me from behind and placed a gentle kiss on my cheek.

"You're back," I said. "What did Romano want this time?"

"Actually, he wanted to congratulate us on our fifth

anniversary, and he expects me to send him photos of our baby girl as soon as she's born."

"That's really nice of him."

Even though Romano called all the time so Oliver could still lead his business, I didn't mind because my husband was always with me, and we were safe here.

Most people didn't even know where he was. His enemies believed he had a good hiding spot, and the press had mostly forgotten all about him. He was still on the list of one of the richest businessmen and only climbing up.

I placed my hand over my stomach, and Oliver covered my hand with his.

"I didn't think it would feel this way," he said.

"Yeah, I think I recall you calling children investments."

"I was wrong about that, and about a lot of things. These past few years have taught me a lot. But how was I supposed to know? I'd never felt anything like it before. I didn't know any better."

"And now you do." I turned toward him and pressed my lips against his.

"What I don't know is if I'm going to do a good job with our kid. I know nothing about being a good father."

"You'll figure it out. I believe in you."

A smile broke out on his face. "What would I do without you? I love you so fucking much."

"I love you too." I grinned.

Oliver caught my hand, and I intertwined my fingers with his.

I'd been all on my own, but now I had my relatives and my own small family.

And I couldn't be happier about it.

I wasn't afraid of living.

I wasn't afraid of anything anymore.